FOREVER BROKEN

A Talon Pack Novel

CARRIE ANN RYAN

Forever Broken
A Talon Pack Novel
By: Carrie Ann Ryan
© 2019 Carrie Ann Ryan
© 978-1-943123-94-0

Cover Art by Charity Hendry

For more information, please join Carrie Ann Ryan's MAILING LIST.
To interact with Carrie Ann Ryan, you can join her FAN CLUB

PRAISE FOR CARRIE ANN RYAN....

"Carrie Ann Ryan knows how to pull your heartstrings and make your pulse pound! Her wonderful Redwood Pack series will draw you in and keep you reading long into the night. I can't wait to see what comes next with the new generation, the Talons. Keep them coming, Carrie Ann!" – Lara Adrian, New York Times bestselling author of CRAVE THE NIGHT

"Carrie Ann Ryan never fails to draw readers in with passion, raw sensuality, and characters that pop off the page. Any book by Carrie Ann is an absolute treat." – New York Times Bestselling Author J. Kenner

"With snarky humor, sizzling love scenes, and brilliant, imaginative worldbuilding, The Dante's Circle series reads as if Carrie Ann Ryan peeked at my personal wish list!" – NYT Bestselling Author, Larissa Ione

"Carrie Ann Ryan writes sexy shifters in a world full of

passionate happily-ever-afters." – *New York Times* Bestselling Author Vivian Arend

"Carrie Ann's books are sexy with characters you can't help but love from page one. They are heat and heart blended to perfection." *New York Times* Bestselling Author Jayne Rylon

Carrie Ann Ryan's books are wickedly funny and deliciously hot, with plenty of twists to keep you guessing. They'll keep you up all night!" USA Today Bestselling Author Cari Quinn

"Once again, Carrie Ann Ryan knocks the Dante's Circle series out of the park. The queen of hot, sexy, enthralling paranormal romance, Carrie Ann is an author not to miss!" *New York Times* bestselling Author Marie Harte

DEDICATION

*To my first readers, my second readers, my latest readers, and all
the ones in between.
Thank you.*

ACKNOWLEDGMENTS

I never thought I'd get here. Seven books and seven novellas in the Redwood Pack series and then nine books in the Talon Pack series means I've spent my entire author career deep into this world.

I fell in love with the Redwoods, then fell in awe with the Talons.

It's over now.

Well...at least for now.

And I know I couldn't have done it without my team.

Thank you Chelle for everything, and not only my edits.

Thank you Charity for my cover and this theme.

Thank you again to Tara for pushing these books and pushing me to write better.

Thank you Viv for helping me plot something new and a little dangerous.

Thank you to the rest of my team who help me with every single part of this book. We're growing closer together as we keep writing and I love you guys so much.

Thank you to my readers for following me along the way and for being so amazing. I couldn't do this without you.

And once again, thank you Dan. I miss you.

-Carrie Ann

FOREVER BROKEN

In the finale to the award-winning Talon Pack series from NYT bestselling author Carrie Ann Ryan sets, the final Brentwood must find his mate as the war with the Aspens comes to a close.

Cheyenne Liles has watched all of her friends mate into the Talon Pack and have their lives changed forever, one by one. She's stood back, helpless to assist in the war with a rival Pack. But just when she thinks her time with the Talons is over and believes she should move on with her human life, the Aspen Pack Alpha takes matters into his own hands, altering her fate far more than a single mate mark ever could.

Max Brentwood used to be the smiling one, the only Brentwood who was somehow able to save his soul during the last Alpha's reign. But his life was irrevocably changed one fateful day on the battlefield, and he was never the same again. Suddenly, Max is forced to face his future and make a choice when Cheyenne comes into danger: let fate decide, or watch his world crumble around him.

The shifters of this world have fought demons, humans, and themselves. Now, it's time to find out who they truly are as the war between the Packs ends, and the moon goddess finally takes a stand.

MOON GODDESS

Change came with time, that was something she had learned long ago. The world as they knew it wouldn't be without change. Under another moon, another blanket of stars, she had chosen the first warrior.

The first hunter, who had broken his own laws— broken the laws of nature and pride.

And when she took his soul, only to force it to share space with that of the wolf he had killed, she had known change would come.

It always did.

When she made the first shifter, she had known the change to come would alter the world, but since she wasn't a goddess of pure prophecy like her sisters, she hadn't known the true extent of her actions. They, these new warriors, had been the ones she needed to make, and her sisters had understood. Some had said it was her destiny.

She was the moon goddess, the one who changed the world—much like each of her sisters had. But she was special.

She had watched her progeny grow and spread throughout the world. She'd witnessed them overcome great hardship and defeat great evil.

The demon that had come from beneath the earth had threatened it all, and yet her shifters had prevailed. They had made their choices well, and in doing so, had created a new life for so many. Their offspring had saved the world, and she knew if they were to survive, their children's children would likely need to do much the same.

Her shifters had kept their secrets, had survived because of it, but now...the world had changed. Because, as she'd said, time moved on and change came with it.

She hadn't made good choices, nor had she made bad. That was on the Pack, the individual. She had taken the soul of one who made a bad decision and forced him to see the horror he wrought.

That had made the man see the good, *be* the good.

But *she* hadn't forced that change.

He had.

And now, those who were *good,* and those who were *bad,* were on opposite sides of a war that should never be.

There were more forces at work, more gods and goddesses, more than merely she and her children. But she knew that when the change came, what was right and what was *needed* might not prevail.

The Alpha who called himself the Supreme of all, a title that held no value without the strength and power behind it, possessed something he shouldn't. How he found it, she didn't know, but it shouldn't be in play at all.

And now, because of it, she would have to change herself.

She knew what she had to do.

She knew what must come.

But when she made a choice, when the change finally came, she didn't know what would be left standing in the ashes at the end.

She wasn't the prophecy-sighted one of her sisters, wasn't the goddess who could see what was to come.

But she could see death in the eyes of her children. Could see the demise of all the people surrounding them.

Because of something that shouldn't be.

So, when the next change came, she, the moon goddess of old, would make her choice.

She just prayed to the others surrounding her that it wouldn't be too late.

And that the cost of the change wouldn't mean everything.

CHAPTER ONE

Blood roared in Cheyenne Lyon's ears, but she didn't scream. If she did, *he* would win. And if he won, then all would be lost. It wasn't just her life she held back her pain for, but the lives of her friends. The only family she had ever known.

This shouldn't be how it turned out.

She was supposed to be safe away from the world that had darkened around her, away from the fighting and magic that were so far out of her depth. The things that she, a woman of science, had no hope of truly comprehending.

The man behind her that wasn't truly a man lowered his head to breathe on her neck, sending chills racing down her spine. These weren't the chills of anticipation that came from being with a lover. Instead, they represented the dread that came from death, that portended the uncertainty of her own fate.

"It's almost ready. Soon, you won't have to wait for what's to come. Soon, you'll do your duty, and the next steps will be taken."

Cheyenne closed her eyes, swallowing the bile that rose in her throat. She didn't want to be here, didn't want to know why Blade, the Alpha of the Aspen Pack, wanted her. But she knew she didn't have a choice.

She was stronger than the tears burning in her eyes, stronger than the need to run and hide from the monsters that lurked in the dark. At least that's what she'd always told herself when she stood by her friends' sides as they each found their mates and became part of the Talon Pack; thereby, somehow becoming enemies of the Aspen Pack.

Enemies of Blade.

Cheyenne had fought alongside her friends and their new people, their new wolves and lions and witches, as she tried not to end up bleeding and dead because she was a mere human in the world of the supernatural. She'd kicked and screamed and tried to fight when she been too weak but had prevailed. The others, however, had been far too strong for her to defeat on her own. She'd stabbed and killed when one of the Talons, Max, a man who was now family to her friends, helped her.

He'd helped her.

But he wasn't here to help her now.

She swallowed hard, aware that Blade still stood behind her, either waiting for her to say something or just wanting to hear himself speak. She had to focus on him, had to concentrate on the present and not what she'd done in the past or who she'd fought alongside.

Cheyenne was a vet, she took care of animals and those who couldn't take care of themselves. Now, she was surrounded by those who could turn into wolves and other creatures she didn't know and didn't want to think about. Her friends had said there might be more out there than wolves, witches, and cat shifters, but she'd tried to put that out of her mind.

She'd always been on the outside looking in. One by one—first Dawn, then Aimee, then Dhani—her friends had found themselves deep in the world of darkness and change. And though Cheyenne had only recently discovered the existence of magic and shifters along with the rest of the human world, somehow, she'd been fully ensconced in it thanks to her friends.

But she wasn't a shifter, wasn't a witch. She hadn't even reacted to the wards like the others had, either feeling the magic too much like Aimee or feeling it differently the way Dhani had. Instead, Cheyenne had felt nothing. She didn't understand the lure of magic and only liked science and indisputable evidence. And while the world beneath her world, or rather the world that now ran *alongside* hers intrigued her, she wasn't part of it.

Her friends would one day move on from her more

than they already had. She was still aging, while they were not. They were starting new lives, maybe even beginning families and growing into their new powers, strengths, and matings.

And Cheyenne wasn't part of any of that.

As the last of her friends mated into the Talon Pack, Cheyenne had told herself she was okay, that she would find a way to move on and stay settled within the human world. She'd convinced herself that she'd be able to fade into memory as her friends physically stayed the same age, and she died a natural, human death.

As Blade breathed down her neck again, standing silently behind her, waiting for something unknown to her, she pulled herself out of those thoughts.

Because there would be nothing natural about her death today.

She didn't know why Blade held her, and he wasn't being forthcoming about his reasons. Maybe it was because she was the weakest link when it came to the Talons. She might not be a member, but since she'd fought alongside Max and had close friends within the den, maybe Blade saw those connections and thought she was worth something.

Only she wouldn't be. She wasn't a mate to any of the Talons or even the Redwoods—another Pack of shifters with deep ties to the Talons. She wouldn't be able to fight back because she didn't have a weapon and, unlike her friends, she wasn't a weapon herself.

"It's almost ready," Blade repeated, then moved to start pacing around the small room he had her in.

She didn't know what *it* was, but she knew she likely wouldn't live when it was ready. She didn't know how she knew that, other than a feeling deep down that this was the end for her, no matter how hard she fought.

Her head ached, and she swallowed hard, not relaxing because even though Blade was no longer directly behind her, he was still close enough to rip out her throat on a whim. She'd been leaving her vet's office late, after hours, her back already hurting from an emergency sock removal surgery on a lovable Lab with far too much energy, when someone had come up from behind and put their hand over her mouth.

She'd screamed, kicked, and tried to use her keys to claw herself free like she'd been taught in not only her self-defense classes but also from Kameron, Dhani's mate. He was the Enforcer of the Talon Pack and had wanted Cheyenne and her friends to know moves to protect themselves. Only her training hadn't been as thorough as the others' since she didn't have claws or fangs to fight back with. Instead, she'd used her body weight to try and throw the man off balance, but it hadn't worked.

He'd been so much stronger than her, and the more she fought, the harder he pulled and squeezed.

Then, he'd knocked her out with the back of his hand on her face, a shocking slap that had set her ears to ringing and had her teeth practically moving in her gums.

When she woke up, she'd been chained to a chair, a dimly lit bulb flickering above her. She'd been alone, cold, but thankfully still clothed. Her cheek stung, and she knew she probably had a concussion.

None of that mattered though when Blade stepped into the room.

She remembered his face, recalled the look of him as he prowled toward her. She'd seen him on the news, had spotted him in person when she fought by Max's side, trying to keep both of them alive even though she knew she wasn't that much help.

Blade was evil incarnate, a true horror in every sense of the word. He'd lost his witch in the last fight, and Cheyenne knew that had cost him. Scarlett had apparently helped him cross the lines of dark magic and move into the area where someone could lose their soul if they weren't careful. He'd tried to get at the Talons for numerous things over the past few years and had nearly succeeded in wiping them out.

Blade had sent rogues over the boundary lines, willing away their need to survive and instilling in them a need to kill. He'd made those rogues break their bonds with their former Packs and had hurt them, forcing them to do what he wanted. He'd kidnapped and tortured Cheyenne's friends, attempting to use them much like he might be using her now: as a symbol of how weak he thought the Talons were. He'd attacked the Pack with magic, taunted them, and used the human media to prey on them, as well.

He'd broken so many edicts, yet he was still free because he and those in his Pack were stronger than the Talons and the Redwoods—possibly stronger than any other Pack and the humans put together. According to Cheyenne's friends, Blade wasn't afraid to use dark magic and risk the end of the world in order to get what he wanted. And because the Talons couldn't do that without killing their own like Blade was unafraid to do, they were at a disadvantage.

And just a few days earlier, he'd declared himself the Supreme Alpha of all the other Packs around the world.

Cheyenne had no idea what that meant, only that it wouldn't be good for her, not with the way Blade had looked at her when he first walked into the small room, and certainly not with the way he stalked toward her now.

Blade had kept her in the chair, the chains loose enough that if she wiggled just right, she might be able to get herself free. But he must have known that when he chained her up. It was all psychological. Because, if she got herself out, she wouldn't be able to get past him. And if, somehow, he tripped or happened to be looking the other way for just the instant she'd need to get through that door, she then had to hope it was unlocked.

If it weren't, then Blade would kill her, or wait to murder her until *it* was ready.

Whatever *it* was.

Even if she got past that door, she didn't know what was on the other side. She didn't know who was out there or where she was. She was probably on Aspen Pack land, but according to the others, not all of the Aspens were on the side of their Alpha. Not all of them agreed with the extent of their Alpha's depravity. Even the Talon's contact, the Beta of the Aspens, Audrey, hadn't been heard from in weeks, making them all worry that Blade had found out about Audrey's clandestine meetings with the Talons and her true loyalties.

Blade hadn't taken Cheyenne's phone, but it was deep in her jacket pocket, and she couldn't reach it. She didn't know if he was unaware that she had it because he and his men hadn't searched her, or if he knew she had it and didn't care.

Because he knew she had no hope of escape.

No chance of rescue because no one knew she was gone.

How could they? She lived alone, worked late, and no one cared where she was at night. They all assumed that she was safely tucked in bed and far away from the world of the Packs and the war surrounding them.

Only, she wasn't.

And the idea of hope was getting a little harder to grasp onto with each passing moment.

"Do you know why you're here?" Blade asked, coming around to face her. His hair was getting a little long, sliding over his forehead and into his eyes. He absently brushed it back as he bent down in front of her. His breath smelled of peppermint, his teeth were perfectly straight, and if he weren't an egotistical maniac with a homicidal streak bent on world domination, she might have considered him attractive. As it was, he reminded her of what she'd imagine a demon might look like.

Smooth moves, and a slick attitude.

The bearer of death.

"No, I don't know why I'm here," she bit out. She wasn't slurring, and though her head hurt, she didn't see double, so she didn't think he'd drugged her. Why would he need to drug her when he could overpower her in an instant?

He glared.

"Why don't you tell me?" She knew she shouldn't have an attitude with him, but what did she have to lose? She wasn't getting out of this room alive. She knew that. There was no amount of magic or prayers to a goddess she wasn't sure she believed in that could save her.

This was it.

And if she were going down, she would do it with a fight. A fight for her life, and a fight for the woman who Cheyenne was beyond the woman in chains.

Blade grinned, but it didn't reach his eyes. No, those eyes were dead, evil, and she didn't know why the media had believed him when he went on air pretending to be a human to put the Talons under fire. There was nothing human about Blade. There was nothing good about him.

"You should know, usually, I'd never turn down a good monologue, but we don't have a lot of time. I've been waiting years for this moment, for the moon to rise at the perfect angle on the one night when the power is the greatest—for the moon goddess to bless me with what is needed."

Cheyenne had no idea what he was talking about, but whatever it was, she knew it could mean death for the Talons, the end of her friends. That was what this man, this wolf, seemed to want—at least in her opinion.

"You're going to serve a specific purpose, Cinnamon."

"It's Cheyenne," she bit out.

"Does it matter?"

"It does to me." She met his gaze and didn't drop her chin when his wolf came into his eyes. She only knew it was that because the others had told her, and she had seen it with the Talons. A gold rim glowed around his iris, pulsating with power. Blade was not a lower-ranking wolf. He'd become Alpha because of his strength, or at least because of his family line—she wasn't sure on the mechanics of it all—but she knew an Alpha couldn't be weak.

And Blade wasn't weak.

He snorted after a moment, then continued. "I searched for over a century for the artifact and then waited a few decades longer to work out the details. And you're the final detail."

He paused, and she swallowed hard, knowing that she wouldn't like what he had to say next. Of course, she hadn't liked any of it. And though her pulse raced, and she practically shook in her chains, she listened to every word and knew that if, somehow, by the grace of the goddess, Cheyenne found a way to survive, she'd tell the Talons everything she knew.

Because she might not be a Pack member, might not be a shifter, but she'd die before she let her friends get hurt because of this monster.

"The artifact needs you. Well, it needs *blood* to activate. And the fact it will be *your* blood will be killing two birds with a single stone."

He pulled out a long, thin knife. Cheyenne thought it might be called a stiletto, but she wasn't sure.

"Actually, a single blade will work." He winked. "Pun not intended."

Then he stood up, and she screamed, pulling herself out of her chains as she bent down and wiggled. His eyes widened a fraction, but then he schooled his features and came at her. She screamed again, trying to duck out of his hold, but he was too fast. He was always too quick.

He pulled her by the hair, the stiletto close to her neck. She froze, leaning against his chest as she tried not to rock forward onto the blade.

"Come with me." He growled the words and tugged her out the door, unlocking it with a key as he did.

She wouldn't have made it, wouldn't have escaped, no matter how hard she fought.

She didn't want to die today.

But it didn't look like she was going to have a choice.

The moon was just dimming in the sky, the sun about to rise on the horizon. She must have been unconscious for longer than she thought if a new day was about to start.

She wasn't going to die on a Sunday but a Monday—a thought she'd never thought to have. Blade pulled her close, the bile in her throat so strong that she was afraid she'd throw up right on his shirt.

"The moon needs to be on her way from the sky and into the darkness, for the light must come." Blade smiled, and Cheyenne knew tears were falling down her cheeks.

She tugged at his hold, trying to get away, but she couldn't.

"You will be our salvation. Blood for blood. Blade for flesh. Sacrament for death."

Then, he slid the blade under her ribs, puncturing her lung but not her heart. She was a vet, had gone to school to learn the anatomy of animals, but she had learned the anatomy of humans, as well.

She knew he'd stabbed her there on purpose so she would bleed out slowly, death taking longer than the seconds or minutes of agony she might have otherwise endured. With her lung punctured, she would lose the ability to breathe, would drown in her own fluids even as her lifeblood left her.

She could already feel her breathing become labored, feel her lungs fighting for oxygen.

Then, she was on her back, blood slowly pooling

around her as Blade stood above her. The moon was still overhead, the sun slowly rising behind Blade's back.

And in his hands, he held a stone, hand-carved and almost brick-shaped, but she couldn't tell what it was exactly. Power leached from him as he squeezed it, his hands covered in her blood. The hairs on her arms stood on end and it felt as if she were too close to a lightning strike. And though the power had to be coming from the stone and into him, it was as if he had so much in him now, he couldn't contain it all.

Then she closed her eyes, afraid that this was the end because it hurt to breathe, it hurt to see the power in his hands. Because she wouldn't be the only one who died for what he held.

When Cheyenne opened her eyes again, Blade was gone, and the only thing she could hear was the wheezing of her breaths. She swallowed hard, slowly reaching into her pocket for her phone. She might not be able to save herself tonight, but maybe she could save her friends.

Her fingers slid over the screen, her blood making it too slippery for her to see the display clearly. She tried to call the last person in her recents, but it scrolled a bit farther and dialed someone she'd only called once—and just so he could have her number.

It had been done in an odd sense of friendship, camaraderie.

Now, she just hoped he answered.

"Cheyenne?" Max growled into the phone. "Where are you?"

"Here," she wheezed. But she knew it was too late, he wouldn't be able to hear her. "I'm here."

She could have sworn she heard a howl as she closed her eyes again, and when she opened them once more, she knew she had to be dreaming.

Max. She didn't actually say the word, didn't have the breath in her lungs.

She only knew it was him hovering over her on three legs, blood on his muzzle, and the anger of a thousand suns in his gaze. During the final battle with the rogue humans who had wanted the wolves to die, Max had lost the lower part of his right arm as well as a lot of flesh on his chest. His chest had healed, but his arm hadn't grown back. Shifter genetics didn't do that. So, in wolf form, he stood on three legs, strong and fierce, though she knew he didn't feel that way.

Max growled, and she wondered why he had blood on his muzzle.

Then, she didn't wonder anymore when he bit into her flesh.

And again.

She didn't scream, didn't feel a thing. She didn't know why she didn't feel anything, she wasn't cold enough to be that close to death, not yet.

Something was protecting her.

And she knew Max wasn't trying to eat her. No, he was attempting to change her, to save her.

He was doing the only thing he could.

And he hadn't given her a choice. If she lived through this, she would make sure he understood that she would have said yes to a change. He was breaking the law, and possibly breaking part of himself to do this, and he already had enough on his shoulders.

She didn't want him to blame himself for this.

But as he bit her again, something snapped inside her. Not physically. But a warmth in her heart spread and seemed to spear outward toward Max. She gasped, suddenly able to breathe as Max quickly changed to his human form—far too fast for him or any other wolf.

Before she could think, he had her in his naked lap and was holding her close, blood covering them both. She couldn't quite understand it all.

"Mate," he whispered. "The moon goddess." He coughed. "Mate."

And then, she fell into the darkness again, wondering if the word *mate* was the last thing she'd ever hear.

Because she wasn't a wolf.

She didn't know if she was Pack.

But...she was Max Brentwood's mate.

Somehow.

CHAPTER TWO

Max Brentwood held Cheyenne in his arms, his body shaking just as much as hers. His wolf pushed at him, wondering what the fuck was going on. The man inside him also wondered that, but it wasn't like he could stand up and yell at the sky to see if the moon goddess might actually talk to him and let him in on the secret.

Though both of them were covered in blood, the wounds he'd added to Cheyenne by biting into her flesh were now gone, healed as if they had never been. If he weren't still able to taste her blood on his tongue, he would have thought he imagined the whole thing. Dreamt the stark fear that had run through his body like a freight train, slamming into him at the sight of her lying still on the grass, blood all around her, the scent of death clinging to her, and the sharp, raspy gasps of breath that she'd fought for.

He'd been in wolf form when he found her, able to run faster on three feet as a wolf than as a human on two. He hadn't been able to take any time to think through his decision, or even hope to hell she wouldn't hate him when —not *if*—she woke up as a wolf. He hadn't known if he was dominant enough to bring on the change. It took someone being near death—something Cheyenne clearly had been —and multiple bites by a wolf in animal form to force the change. It was damn illegal now thanks to human laws, and not something done often, according to Pack law.

Forcing a shift wasn't done.

But he hadn't cared.

He'd had to save her. Part of him might have thought it was only because her friends were family now, Pack. But, maybe, part of him had known that even though he was broken and couldn't feel a damn thing when it came to magic and the moon goddess anymore since the battle with the humans...maybe he'd known deep down that she was *his*.

He'd bitten her, praying to a goddess he hadn't prayed to in far too long. Praying that the enzyme would take. Praying Cheyenne would survive the bite. Praying she would survive the change. He hadn't been able to stop the bleeding in the wound in her side, hadn't been able to heal the bruising on her face and throat.

And when she opened her eyes, gasping out words, his heart had nearly stopped. Then, the world had shifted, and so had he. He'd never changed to human form that quickly in his life. Even his cousin and Alpha, Gideon, didn't shift that fast.

Suddenly, he was in human form, and Cheyenne looked like she would survive.

Someone had intervened, and Max had a feeling it had to do with the goddess he'd prayed to, the one he'd thought had forsaken him when his life was on the line and he lost part of himself, part of his soul, and part of his wolf.

Now, he had Cheyenne resting on his right upper arm, using his left hand to search her body for any cuts or bites he might have missed. There was enough blood under them at this point that he knew she'd lost a good portion of hers, enough that if whatever—or *whoever*—had intervened were just a moment later, Cheyenne would have been gone before he found her.

When he found nothing, something that worried the hell out of him considering what he'd seen just a few moments ago, he let out the breath he hadn't known he was holding and reached for her phone. He'd lost his clothes when he shifted to get to her as fast as he could after her phone call.

They'd started searching for her once Kameron's patrols found out she hadn't gotten home the night before, and her car had been left at her now-closed clinic.

He'd been irrationally anxious and angry about anything happening to the one person who should have been safe. Cheyenne wasn't a wolf, she wasn't *anything* having to do with the Talon Pack, other than a friend to those within the den walls.

She should have been *safe*.

He growled again, then made the call to Kameron since it was the first of his family he saw in Cheyenne's contacts. It was good that she had so many of them in there for emergencies, but he'd known that she was trying to cut ties with the Pack. He'd seen it in her eyes at the last event she'd been to. He'd been in the corner, keeping away from the others because he hadn't wanted his bad mood to piss off his family...but he'd watched her.

He always watched her.

He'd been drawn to her from the start, though he hadn't known why. She hadn't been his mate—his wolf would have told him. He'd known he was broken, but he'd also known that he wasn't *that* broken.

Now, he knew.

He hadn't been able to feel her for a reason.

But he also knew that she wanted to walk away from everything having to do with the Pack. And he'd understood. Those who were part of his den, part of his family, had almost been killed, they had been sent to hell and back. His body and his wolf were proof of that.

Cheyenne had wanted to walk away.

And now, she couldn't.

He quickly made the call, disconnecting once Kameron told him they were on their way and Cheyenne finally stirred.

"Max?" Her lips barely moved, but he heard the words, so he leaned forward, brushing his own lips across her forehead. He didn't know what else to do, and he was a wolf, touch usually helped with anxiety—not that he touched people often these days, but this wasn't about him, this was about Cheyenne.

"I'm here," he whispered. He needed to move her, needed to get her off this land. It might be neutral, but that didn't mean eyes weren't watching. He'd been able to scent the one responsible, even if he hadn't wanted to put two and two together because then he'd have a face for the person who dared come at Cheyenne.

Blade hadn't taken her to Aspen land, the Alpha was far too crafty for that. If it hadn't been for Max's wolf going on instinct, and Cheyenne's phone call, he might have been too late.

"Good."

Then, she was out again, and the others were running through the trees, some on four legs, Kameron and a couple of others on two. As soon as his family arrived, Max stood up in one movement. He might be missing part of an arm, but he'd learned to compensate for balance. He was still far stronger than any human, and most wolves. He was a dominant, a shifter with the power to be in the hierarchy or even an Alpha of a small Pack—just like any of his family members.

Kameron met his gaze, their eyes the same deep blue that all of the Brentwoods shared. Kameron was his cousin, his Enforcer. Max was the only one of his generation without a title. It hadn't bothered him before, and with Cheyenne in his arms, hurt and weak, it didn't bother him now.

"Do you know what happened?" Kameron asked, his gaze roaming over the area.

"No, but I'll find out. And when I do? Blade's dead. That's his scent."

Kameron gave him a tight nod. "He deserves to be dead five times over. At least. And I can scent you on her, you know. What the fuck happened?"

Max pulled Cheyenne closer, aware that he was still naked, but he didn't care, not when there were more important things going on. "Let's get her safe and cleaned up. Then, we'll talk."

Kameron looked like he wanted to ask more but just shook his head. "Let me hold her for a minute while you pull on the pants Ryder is about to give you. You can't run through this land to the closest road with your dick hanging out, holding a blood-covered woman."

Max flipped him off, then handed Cheyenne to his cousin. It was only because Kameron was mated that Max's wolf even allowed that to happen. It didn't make any sense, and it wouldn't to a human, but his wolf knew who his mate was, and he and Cheyenne had a fully blooded bond between them now.

They hadn't completed the two steps needed, but *someone* had circumvented the rituals. It required a bite on the shoulder to connect the wolf, a mating mark. It took sex between the two or three mates, spilling seed or an orgasm to join the human halves. That was how it had always worked, yet he knew the mating rules had changed over the past few years as humans, demons, witches, and the moon goddess herself interfered in their matings.

Max shoved his legs into the pants Ryder handed over, thankful that they were sweats so he didn't have to deal with buttoning them. He could do it one-handed, but the stress and anger rolling through his system currently would likely make him clumsy.

Kameron handed Cheyenne back over, and then Max was on the run, his mate in his hold, and his wolf at the front of his consciousness.

Everything had changed, and he didn't know what was going to happen next. But, then again, it didn't matter. He'd do what was needed, he always did. He just hoped to hell that Cheyenne wouldn't once again be caught in the crossfire.

CHAPTER THREE

Max sat by Cheyenne's bed, waiting for her to wake up. Maybe if he scowled at her more, she'd finally open those eyes and stop giving his wolf reason to growl. Walker and Leah had been in and out of the room and hadn't shoved Max out, so he figured he must look ready to murder someone.

Considering that he'd shown up at the nearest Pack SUV covered in sweat and blood with a woman in his arms and then hadn't let go of her until he met up with his cousin and Healer, Walker...he didn't blame them for thinking that.

He *was* ready to murder someone.

The woman in the bed near him didn't scent of wolf, only the one who'd hurt her. The shift hadn't taken, then again, something had come in and changed it all.

Leah, Ryder's mate and a healer in her own right since

she was a strong water witch, had taken one look at him and handed over a wet towel so he could wipe his face and chest. He'd thought it would be enough to make it so he didn't look *that* dangerous.

He might be wrong about that.

Leah had given him a once-over, probably ensuring that none of the blood was his, and then left the room. He figured that she or Walker would be back in soon to check on him and Cheyenne. They were worried about him just as much as they were about Cheyenne because nothing was right about this picture.

Somehow, Max had a mate, and that mate, who had been drowning in her own blood earlier that morning, was now almost completely healed and resting.

None of it made sense, and they still had no idea what it had to do with Blade.

Because it always had to do with Blade these days.

Cheyenne mumbled something in her sleep, her hands fisting in the sheets beside her. Max stood up, ignoring the ache in his hips from his run. He was faster than he'd ever been, stronger than he'd ever been because he had to become that man. But, sometimes, he strained himself from pushing too hard. He'd get over it.

When Cheyenne moaned again, he reached out and put his hand over hers, knowing that when his wolf got out of hand, he needed touch—even if the man wanted nothing to do with it.

Cheyenne might not be a wolf, but she'd been pumped

full of magic to the point where he could still taste it on his tongue, feel the weight of it in his soul—and not just through the fragile bond pulsating between the two of them in rhythm with their heartbeats.

As soon as he touched her, Cheyenne calmed down, but when he moved away again to give her space, she thrashed. They hadn't been able to wake her up, and Walker said it was because she needed to finish healing what was inside and that it would take time.

The fact that Walker could feel that along the tentative bond told them all that Cheyenne was now Pack, even if not fully because Gideon hadn't blooded her into the Pack itself yet. Not that all of the current Pack members had needed Gideon since extenuating circumstances had led to new additions over the past few years. But when Max had tried to turn Cheyenne wolf to save her—something that clearly hadn't taken since he could only smell his wolf on her—everything had changed.

He didn't know what would happen next, but things were well on their way to becoming complicated.

"You should hold her," Walker said softly as he came into the room. Max had known his cousin was behind him since his wolf had heard him long before Walker showed up, but Max still hadn't turned toward the door. Instead, he'd focused on Cheyenne and the pain he couldn't take away.

"Why?" he asked, his voice hoarse.

"Because she's your mate. I don't know how it

happened, and I know you don't either. That's something we'll figure out, Max. We've figured out weirder things when it comes to this Pack and family."

This time, Max snorted, looking over his shoulder at the Healer. "Truer words have never been spoken."

"Hold her, Max. She needs you. We'll figure out the rest when she wakes up. The den is already on alert in case something else comes, and the media isn't aware of what happened to her as far as we can tell. We're keeping an eye on her clinic, and moved her car here so that no one gets suspicious. We're working on the small things so you can help her wake up. But hold her, Max. Hold your mate."

It felt weird to hear those words. Max hadn't thought he'd get a mate, not after watching each of his family members find theirs one by one and him being left behind...again.

He gave his cousin a tight nod, then slowly slipped into the large hospital bed that could fit wolf and human easily. He wrapped his arm around Cheyenne, careful not to jostle her, and she immediately leaned into him, putting her hand over his heart, over the scars which had healed but that he could still feel with each intake of breath.

Walker left them alone, and Max pulled up the blanket so she was covered. Her breathing eased, and it looked as if she were sleeping after a long night of work, not after a magical and violent set of events Max couldn't quite comprehend.

He'd thought he died once before and had woken up a

broken shell of who he once was. It hadn't mattered that he'd lost part of himself physically. Contrary to what the others thought, he knew that didn't make him any less than who he was before. He'd learned to work around the missing part of his arm, and while it might take him longer to perform certain tasks, he could do almost anything now with a few modifications.

The scars on his chest had healed from where the human who had wanted to control all wolves and wipe them from the face of the Earth had stabbed him over and over and over again. Max had been blown to his back from a bomb during the battle, and when he came to, the human man had stood over him, his sanity long gone as he ravaged Max's chest.

He'd pierced Max's heart, his lungs, most of his organs.

And because Max had been bleeding out already from losing his arm in the explosion, and had a concussion on top of it, he hadn't been able to fight back.

He remembered every stab of the knife, every twist, every ache, but he didn't remember how it had started. Only that he'd woken up to hell.

He'd thought he would die. Thought that the last face he saw would be the man who killed him.

Walker had saved him. The others had helped.

And Max had been brought back from the brink of death. But not the same. How could he be the same when he and his wolf were broken, not just physically but spiritually...mentally?

He'd never thought to have a mate. There was something *wrong* inside him. What could he offer a mate? But it seemed the moon goddess had other plans for him. Schemes that included the woman in his arms, no matter the choices the two of them might have made.

Cheyenne mumbled, and he looked down at her, forcing those thoughts from his mind. He'd figure out what to do with them later. First, he needed to focus on Cheyenne.

Who, thankfully, had woken up, and now sat staring at him with those grey eyes of hers that always captivated him—even if he hadn't wanted to think too hard about it before.

"Max?"

Her voice was even more hoarse than his, and he leaned down, doing the only thing he could think of. He brushed his lips against her forehead. "Don't speak. Let me get you some water for your throat."

Her hands tightened on his shirt, and he froze.

"Or I can call my cousin in to help."

She just blinked at him, and the bond between them flared. He couldn't feel what she was feeling, their connection was far too new for that, and he didn't know what kind of bond they would share anyway. But the fact that her eyes widened told him that she felt the difference, as well.

That was something they would have to work on. Somehow.

Walker walked in, his pleasant Healer face on, even though Max knew that his cousin was worried about them both. Hell, the whole Pack was worried with war on the mind, and Blade's announcement about being Supreme Alpha—whatever *that* meant—far too new for comfort.

"You're awake. That's good. Let me get you some water to help your throat." He tapped his ear as Cheyenne gave Max and then Walker a weird look. "Wolf hearing. I was already on my way in when Max offered to call for me. Why don't you stay in bed, Max? You're keeping her heart rate down." He paused, looking at Cheyenne. "Unless you'd rather him leave the room. It's all up to you, Cheyenne."

She shook her head, and Max frowned, a sense of disappointment washing over him even though he tried to ignore the cause of it. Sure, they might be mated, but neither of them had made the choice to do so. So the idea that he was sad that his mate was rejecting him shouldn't hurt. They weren't really mates. Or, maybe they were, but they didn't know each other enough for the pain to make sense.

And maybe Max needed time to breathe because he was thinking himself into circles.

"I...I'm fine." Max let out a low growl at the sound of the pain in her voice, and she froze in his hold, her hand still resting on his chest.

"Sorry. Didn't mean to startle you."

She shook her head, then took a sip of the water

Walker handed Max. She licked her lips, and Max did his best not to look at those lips. It was his wolf and the mating bond making him act this way, it couldn't be anything else. Not when they were in this position because of something out of their control. She hadn't had a choice in the matter and that meant there would be no acting on any urge.

Ever.

"It was the first time I *felt* a growl."

He nodded, understanding. "Different for you then?"

She nodded. "You could say that." She coughed, and he gave her more water, careful that she didn't spill. "I need to tell you what happened...though I don't know *everything*."

Cheyenne looked over at Walker, then back at Max. "There's something you need to know."

Max had a feeling none of them were going to like what she had to say.

BLADE

Blade looked down at the stone in his hand, the power emanating from it so intense he'd almost dropped it a few times. Not that he'd let anyone know that. After all, he was the *Supreme Alpha*, the highest, strongest, greatest Alpha of all time, and that he could even hold the artifact as he was, was indeed a testament to the fact that he deserved the position and title.

When he'd gone on the special broadcast network where all the Packs in the country and the *world* could get in contact with each other, he'd done it with purpose.

The others needed to know that their salvation, their protection from those who dared tarnish the shifters' name in the world and would allow humans to rule them all was here.

Blade would be that for them.

He'd been that for his Pack.

He'd kept his Pack's secrets about their unusual members from all the other Packs and witches and humans for years. And it was because of his traitorous Beta that the word had gotten out that cat shifters existed.

He'd taken care of Audrey and would soon take care of the others when the time came.

The other Packs needed a leader who could make the tough decisions for them. The weak would tremble and be separated as chaff like they needed to be.

Keen members of his Pack would lead the way in that endeavor as they had aided in his war with the Talons thus far. Blade couldn't deal with each and every detail, so he delegated. Much like he'd allocated things to his witch.

He let out a growl, his hand burning as the artifact within it heated up.

He couldn't believe the Talon trash, and their precious former humans had *killed* his witch. He now knew that he'd relied on Scarlett far too much, and finding another to replace her would take time. But he'd find someone.

After all, as soon as they saw what happened to the wolves who didn't fall in line, the witches would flock to him, eager for his protection.

The other Alphas would know the power he held shortly.

The artifact was *his* now.

The human, Cinnamon or Cheyenne or whatever her name was, was dead, and her blood had given life to the power in his hands. Her death would not be in vain. Her death would pave the way for his ascension and the end of any Alpha who dared go against him.

And before they died, they would lose their power.

He would show them who the *true* power was.

And they would fall to their knees in thanks that he would grant them their lives.

If they begged nicely.

CHAPTER FOUR

Cheyenne found herself sitting in a comfortable living room, blankets piled on top of her since her friends were afraid she'd catch a chill. Though how she could be cold with the furnace that was Max Brentwood sitting near her, she didn't know. She still wasn't exactly sure how she'd found herself on the couch to begin with.

One moment, she'd been saying to Walker and Max that she needed to tell them something important. The next, Walker was checking her out and making sure she was physically okay. And then, she was in Max's hold as he carried her out of the clinic and down the path to the Alpha's house, where there would now be a family meeting that apparently centered around her and everything that had happened.

And while she appreciated that almost everyone would

be here so she didn't have to tell the story more than once, it was all a little intimidating. She was suddenly surrounded by some of the most powerful people in the world...at least in *her* world.

The people she'd thought to walk away from before the pain got to be too much when they were forced to leave her behind, now sat on various couches and cushions on the floor around her, some standing and leaning against walls.

The Brentwoods were not only a big family, they were *big* in general. All of Max's cousins and siblings had wide shoulders and thick muscles. Max was only slightly more slender, but with the way he moved—and yes, she'd watched him move, she hadn't been able to help herself—she knew he had immense power within that body of his.

Even though the females might be smaller in stature, they were stronger than any other group of women Cheyenne knew. The fact that three of them were her best friends in the world only aided in that perception.

"Can you tell us what happened?" Brie, Gideon's mate, asked. She was a submissive wolf, though Cheyenne didn't know what that really meant in the grand scheme of things. Her friends had told her it meant that Brie could soothe even the most dangerous of wolves, and that was clear given that she'd mated a very powerful Alpha wolf.

Of course, thinking about a powerful Alpha wolf made Cheyenne think of Blade, and she shivered.

Max immediately put his arm around her shoulders,

pulling her in close. She watched the others carefully follow the movement, but she wasn't in the mood to deal with what any of that meant. For some reason, when Max touched her, Cheyenne wasn't as nervous or scared. She could still feel all of that, but it wasn't as bad when he was near. It was like something inside her knew that she could handle it because he was there—not dealing with it *for* her, but there nonetheless.

She knew it was the mating bond, the thing she could feel inside her that told her Max was hers. But she was doing her best not to think about the full ramifications of that right then. Or maybe ever, since she wasn't sure she wanted to know what Max thought about it all.

Cheyenne licked her dry lips, and Max reached for the water glass. Although thankful, she shook her head since she was full of water, and he set it back down. It was only then that she realized that he'd slipped his so-called *bad* arm behind her to tug her in, something he'd been careful not to do in the past. He was so good at hiding his injury from the rest of the world, the fact that he wasn't doing so right then was something she would have to think about later...or chalk up to the fact that they were both clearly shaken.

"Cheyenne?"

She mentally shook herself at Brie's gentle nudge and let out a breath. "Sorry. Woolgathering."

"It's understandable," Dawn, her friend and wolf

shifter who happened to be mated to Max's brother, Mitchell, said.

"So...what happened?" Cheyenne shook her head. "I can tell you what happened, the details, but I don't know the *why* of it. Only what I heard him say, or at least think I heard him say."

"Blade." Max said the word, and it didn't sound like a question, but she answered anyway.

"Yes. Blade. I take it you, uh...smelled him on me?"

Max let out a low growl, and so did half of the men in the room. Considering that Blade had either hurt them or their mates, she understood the sentiment.

"Yes."

She nodded. "I was working late on a surgery, and my late-night tech helped me close down the clinic, though she was staying overnight since I had animals in need of care." She froze. "Is Alex okay? Did Blade get her, too?"

Cheyenne had asked Max, but it was Kameron who answered. "We talked to her, she's fine. She doesn't know what happened, and we're keeping a lid on it, though she's curious. That could pose a problem."

Cheyenne stiffened. "A problem for who? Alex is a good person. Protective."

"We know," Dhani put in. "She's just going to keep asking questions that could either get her in trouble with Blade's Pack or get *us* in trouble with the humans because of all the new laws and treaties."

"I'll call her. Can I do that? What about my patients?"

Cheyenne tried to control her breathing. "I have someone that can come in and help with the clinic, but I need to handle all of that. If I didn't show up today..." She closed her eyes and pressed her hands to her face. Cheyenne had been so worried about everyone else, she had forgotten she had an actual job in the human realm where she had people and animals that depended on her.

"Call Alex and whoever you can to come and take care of the clinic," Gideon said, his voice so authoritative it was easy to see why he was the Alpha. He was kind, but his words left no room for disobedience.

"For how long?" she asked.

"Until we figure out what's going on," Max answered softly. "It's not safe until we have a handle on what Blade wants and what's coming next. And until you're back in fighting shape. You'll stay with me until that happens."

Cheyenne froze at that statement, but the others seemed to move on from it.

Aimee walked forward and knelt in front of her. "I'm sorry this is hurting your life, and your world is changing. And if there was any other way, you know the Pack would make it work. The Redwoods have a vet on hand that was married into the Pack recently. The vet is wolf now, but the animals don't seem to mind. Do you want them to try and help you out, as well? Just until we know you're safe and those who work for you and rely on you are, too."

Cheyenne nodded, trying to keep up. Aimee was the

sweetest and most quiet of her friends. The fact that she was now a cat shifter hadn't changed that.

Cheyenne patted her friend's hand, then rolled her shoulders back, trying to get her mind on track. "We'll handle it. If my colleague can't take over my remaining patients and appointments, then I'll ask the Redwood Pack member. But I should get back to my story. I'm sorry for derailing the conversation."

"You have your own life, Cheyenne." Max's voice pulled her toward him, even though she tried to stay ramrod straight so she could find the strength to get through the upcoming conversations. "It's okay that you need to get your affairs in order." He frowned. "And...not how I meant it."

That made her smile. Actually *smile*, even after the night she'd had.

He didn't smile back, but his brow rose. She'd count that as a win. The others were waiting for her story, so she continued.

"I was just headed to my car when someone came at me from behind. I fought back." She looked at Kameron. "I used the moves you taught me, but they weren't enough."

"Not when you're dealing with a wolf. But you fought back," Kameron said sharply. "That counts for more than you want it to."

She nodded. "I know. And I'm grateful that I was able to fight at all. He knocked me out. I don't know if it was

Blade or someone working for him, but I woke up, chained to a chair in a small storehouse or shack. I'm not sure what it was, but that doesn't matter." She paused. "Was it on Aspen land? I assumed so because it was Blade, but then again, I didn't hear anyone else around. Not really. So, I don't know where I was."

"You were on neutral land. At least that's where I found you. I don't know if you were moved there later or not, but with the timeline we're looking at, Blade took you to the storehouse directly from your clinic parking lot."

"Well, that's good to know since I hate the fact that I don't remember every moment." She looked at everyone who was clearly trying not to look at her directly and was grateful that Walker had kept her medical status private. He was a Healer, not a doctor, and she didn't know the rules. "He didn't violate me that way, even during the times I don't remember."

Every single person relaxed marginally, even Max by her side.

"I woke up in the storehouse," she continued, needing to get the story over with. "He'd chained me to a chair, but loosely. I don't know if he wanted me to think I could get out and psych myself out about it or if he was that stupid."

"I wouldn't put it past him either way," Kameron mumbled, and that made her snort.

"That was my thinking too, and I don't even know him as well as you do. Anyway, he went on and on about how I was going to help him finish his grand plan." She tried to tell them every single word she remembered and was grateful that someone was writing it down so she didn't have to do it herself. "Then, he came after me, and I tried to get out. Only he dragged me outside." She closed her eyes, and Max squeezed her hand. She held onto him like a lifeline.

"You can take a break if you need to," Max whispered.

"No, I'm fine. Really. He said he needed the moon to fade but used pretty words that sounded like he'd read them somewhere. Then, he stabbed me with a thin, sharp knife that I think is called a stiletto or something. He got me right under the ribs and punctured my lung, but not my heart or any other vital organ." She put her hand over where the wound had been, the wound that she no longer bore.

"I thought I was dead. Then, he took this stone I hadn't seen before and put my blood on it. I know he said some other things, but I don't remember them. I just know he left me there to die and took the stone that felt of *power* away. I don't know what it was or what it will do, but I *know* it means bad news for the Packs—and maybe the whole world. He used my blood to do something, and I have no idea what it means."

They had her describe the stone, and she gestured for a pad of paper and pen, drawing what she remembered to the best of her abilities. She wasn't the best artist, but she'd done enough anatomy diagrams in her life to know her way around paper and a pencil.

"Before we get into the whys and whats of what happened, there's something we need to talk about." Gideon pinched the bridge of his nose as he spoke.

You're healed," Walker said. "I didn't have to Heal you. And from what Max said, you weren't healed when he got there."

"I don't know what happened," she said quickly.

Max sighed. "I tried to change her." He looked at Cheyenne. "I'm sorry for not giving you a choice, sorry for all the pain I caused. But I couldn't let you die like that, and the only thing I knew that could possibly help was to force the shift. I took your choice away and broke the law. *All* the laws for that matter. And for that, I'm so damn sorry."

"Don't be sorry," she put in, aware the others were looking at them. "I was thinking as you were doing it that I knew you were going to feel like this was all your fault and you'd have guilt. But you shouldn't. I probably would have done the same thing in your position. I would do *anything* to keep the people around me healthy and alive. So, I get why you did it, and though I don't know what choice I would have made if there had been one, I'm glad you tried." She paused, looking down at herself. "Though it didn't really work out as planned. Did it?"

"I don't know who healed you or who *Healed* you, but I have an idea," Max said, completely ignoring her other words, and for that, she was grateful. That was something

42

they'd have to talk about later in private. Or bury and not talk about at all. She wasn't sure which one she preferred.

"The moon goddess," Gideon added, his voice a growling whisper. "You think it was her."

"She's the only one I know that has that kind of power, the ability to heal someone completely like it never happened *and* create a mating bond." Max looked into Cheyenne's eyes, and she didn't blink. "That's not how mating works, and yet..."

"And yet...here we are."

"Here we are."

"So, what does it all mean?" Dhani asked, thankfully cutting the tension not only in the room but also between Cheyenne and Max.

"I thought the mating bonds were fixed?" Leah asked, leaning into her mate, Ryder. "With everything that has happened, I thought they were back to what they were before the changes."

When, through no fault of their own, the Talons not only added new blood to the Pack but also magical and nonmagical elements, the moon goddess had pulled back from the mating bonds. Apparently, before, one saw another and *knew* who their mate was. Sometimes, it took a few years for their wolves to get to know each other and become the people they needed to be before they were ready to mate, but it always showed up.

That hadn't been the case recently, and not until

Walker and Aimee somehow fixed it for everyone else did people start to sense their future mates again.

"I mean, I felt the potential mating bonds," Dhani put in. "Even when I probably shouldn't have because I was human at the time."

Kameron leaned over and kissed his mate's temple. "You were a witch, even then. And once the magic was back in place, I felt the bonds."

Max growled next to Cheyenne, and she leaned in to him. "The way the bonds can be sensed might be fixed for some, but they clearly weren't for everyone." He paused, his brow furrowed. "Or maybe it was just me."

She hated that he constantly set himself apart from the others, and not just in this instant. No, she'd seen him do it long before this. When they'd first met, he would stand in a corner, away from the others. Watching. Listening. But never participating.

Not knowing what else to do, Cheyenne put her hand on his arm, bringing his attention to her. "Or, it could have been me."

Once again, there was silence, and she cleared her throat.

"Anyway..." She paused. "I don't know what's going to happen with *that*, and, well...I need to think."

Max leaned forward. "And that's something between me and Cheyenne anyway. The important thing to discuss within this group is what we're going to do about Blade and this...artifact of his. What is it, and what does it do?"

Gideon nodded. "We'll have a Pack meeting. The den needs to know what's out there, and with so many of us—including the elders—someone might actually know what Blade is holding."

"That's true," Kameron put in. "Contrary to belief, we don't actually know everything about everything."

Cheyenne held back a smile, the fact she'd almost smiled at all right then surprising her, when Dhani rolled her eyes at her mate.

"We'll have to be cautious," Brie put in, holding her mate's hand. Gideon seemed so large next to his mate, not just in stature, but in presence, but Brie didn't back down. Cheyenne had to remember that. "There have been so many dramatic shifts and changes in the Pack in recent years that some are scared. Uneasy. We're long-lived and, sometimes, those who have lived even longer than those in this room can't handle the changes like we can. It scares them," she repeated. "And scared shifters can lead to things we might not be ready for." She winced after she said it. "I don't mean they need to be cautious of you, Cheyenne."

Cheyenne nodded. "But they might see me as a symbol for all that change—or even *any* of us who have joined the Pack recently. Because they can't see Blade and the Aspens in person, those who aren't on the front lines won't know where to direct their confusion and anger."

Cheyenne had taken enough psychology classes in

college that she had the bare basics down and a fascination with the study outside of her veterinary medicine.

Max didn't move or even lean into her, but she knew that he was somehow closer to her, as if she felt his wolf wanting to protect her. She didn't know why she knew that, and perhaps it had to do with the new, tentative bond between them, but for some reason, she knew she could relax just a fraction because he was near. It was a weird thing to feel after so many years of forcing herself not to rely on anyone, not even her friends that she loved and would sacrifice anything for.

"You'll be safe here," Gideon said, and it was a pronouncement. "I don't know how the bond snapped into place, but it did. You're Pack. I can feel your presence within the threads, and soon, the others who have power will, as well. If they don't already."

Walker cleared his throat. "I do. That's why I was able to tell there was something different with the Healing."

Cheyenne nodded, knowing she looked calm and cool, though inside, she was anything but.

"Cheyenne is tired, and, frankly, so am I," Max said suddenly, and she turned to him, wondering why he was speaking for her. She didn't question him though because she was in a room full of people she knew but which she was also on the periphery of. She wasn't about to make a scene when everyone was already focused on her too much as it was. She'd find her place and figure out what was coming soon, but for now, she'd let Max talk.

"Pack meeting tomorrow," Gideon said.

"The elders will be there," Ryder added.

"Then we will be, too." Max stood up and held out his hand. "Come on. It's been a long day."

The others moved around, standing up and talking amongst each other, some leaving to go pick up their children from the sitter or wherever they were. Cheyenne placed her hand in Max's and stood up, wondering why her fingers tingled when he let go, as if her skin missed his already. It didn't make any sense, and, once again, it reminded her that she wasn't prepared for this magic and the paranormal life she suddenly found herself immersed in.

Dhani, Aimee, and Dawn each hugged her close, surrounding her in a group like they always did when one of them needed it or when the others *thought* they needed it.

"Come, stay at my house," Dhani said.

"Or mine," Aimee and Dawn added together.

She knew the three were worried about what had just happened and, frankly, so was Cheyenne. But, for some reason, she couldn't stay with them. She *needed* to figure out why part of her yearned for Max, even though he was only a few steps away. Something had changed deep inside her, and she wasn't sure she was prepared to face it, but she also wasn't ready to completely ignore it.

"I'll be fine," Cheyenne said after a moment. "I'll see you all in the morning, but..."

Dawn met her gaze and nodded. Dawn had been born a wolf and had lived with the idea of the paranormal and magic and everything that came with it for far longer than the rest of them. Of all of Cheyenne's friends, Dawn would understand. It had been the rest of them who had been forced to learn everything to try and keep up.

"We're here if you need us." Dawn swallowed hard as Cheyenne did the same. "And welcome to the Pack. I just wish it were under better circumstances."

Cheyenne knew Dawn meant the kidnapping and attack, but she hadn't missed the minuscule flinch in the corner of Max's eye. He masked it well, but he had to think Dawn's comment was about him and not everything else. Or, maybe, he hadn't wanted Cheyenne to begin with, and the whole mating thing was a mistake. She needed to sort out her thoughts, and then perhaps she could sort out her feelings. But she couldn't do any of that if she was standing with her friends who were trying to help. She already felt helpless enough.

"Thanks," she said quietly. "I'll see you in the morning." Then she moved through the group and towards Max. He held out his hand once again, and she slid her fingers into his, ignoring the tension radiating from him.

They didn't speak as they walked out of the house and down the path to where he lived.

She had no clothes. No toothbrush. She had nothing of her own with her, and yet she was about to stay at Max's house. Everything had changed, and she had to act as if she was perfectly fine with it. She had no idea what was going to happen with her patients or her home or anything else because she was now irrevocably tied to the Pack and the man beside her—and she didn't even know him.

"You're starting to panic." Max squeezed her hand as they walked into a small two-story home surrounded by trees. The house looked like a perfect place for a family, as if it had been waiting for the next part of Max's life.

Cheyenne had a feeling he'd had it built—or built it himself—before whatever made him look like he was lost happened. The thing that made him the man he was now. Because the Max before the attack had been full of hope, but the man in front of her now looked like he either wanted to hide away or was struggling to keep up.

Since she felt the same, she couldn't blame him.

Cheyenne stood in Max's living room, noticing that it was clean and free of dust, but it didn't look like it was used often. It was like a shell of what it had once been.

"The guest room is upstairs. I don't really have anything for you to wear, but if one of the women doesn't bring you something—though, knowing them, they just might bring you a whole suitcase-worth of things—you can sleep in my shirt for the night." His final words were almost a growl, and it took a moment for her to realize that his wolf liked the idea of her in his clothes. Maybe it had to do with scents and claiming, or perhaps she was too tired to dive too deeply into anything just then.

"Thank you." He turned to face her, and she studied the strong line of his jaw, the way his hair flopped over his forehead when he moved too quickly, and the way his lips thinned as he pressed them together. She knew they had a lot to talk about, and even more to think about, but for now, just the idea that she wasn't surrounded by so many people who cared about her—only the one tied to her in a way she didn't understand yet—made her feel safer than she'd thought possible. "I know I'm in your space, and I have a feeling that's not something you like, but I appreciate it."

He frowned, studying her face. "You seem to know a lot about what I'm thinking for someone who hasn't really talked to me."

She shrugged. "I study people. I can't help it. I want to know the whys. It's part of my job, even though I mostly work with animals. Not that I think shifters are animals..."

That made him quirk a smile. "I know you helped some of the shifters in wolf form when the earthquake hit and during other battles. You're good at what you do. And I fought beside you, remember? I guess we know each other more than I thought."

"And I guess we'll have to learn who we are even more." They were silent for a moment, and she wished she could take back the words. "But for now, I'd really just like to go to bed. I know the rest of the world needs to know what Blade has and, in my world, I need to know what's going on, but I really just want to go to bed."

"Then I'll get you my shirt, and you can sleep. Tomorrow, we'll have more questions, but I know we'll get some answers. We're not going to let too much time pass without them." He leaned forward and brushed his lips across her forehead. It was just a soft caress, not even a full kiss, but her shoulders lowered, and her eyes closed as she inhaled, her entire being calming just with him near.

She didn't understand the reaction and knew from his body language that he was just as confused.

But it didn't matter. Come morning, she would tense up again as she tried to untangle the threads that were her life and that of the Pack, but for now, she would follow Max upstairs to his guest room and go to bed.

The next day would be there all too soon, and she'd have to face her new reality.

No matter how unbelievable and dramatic it seemed.

CHAPTER FIVE

Max woke up before the sun and knew his world had changed. The house smelled of woman, of mate, and yet it was distant enough that his wolf wasn't happy. His other half wasn't angry, as it seemed to be most days since the battle, but it wanted their mate, and since that wasn't happening anytime soon, Max would just deal with whatever his wolf did—like he'd been doing for a while now.

He took his shower and got dressed for the Pack meeting that would happen later that morning at the Pack circle. He had a feeling it wasn't going to go smoothly since they needed to discuss the Supreme Alpha business as well as the artifact. Keeping the latter a secret wasn't an option, not when the knowledge of it could protect the Pack. None of his family knew what it was, but their Pack was deeply knowledgeable and talented, and someone down the line could have read about it over the past century or two. Max had a feeling the elders would know, and they were coming to the meeting. Sometimes, the elders didn't join in on discussions like this since they were far too old to deal with the daily issues of the Pack, their minds full of so many memories that sometimes they found themselves lost in their heads and not truly living in the present.

Max was over a hundred and fifty years old and had his own memories he sometimes drowned in, but it paled in comparison to that of the elders. And though the Pack's elder ranks had thinned over the years thanks to war, the betrayal of the previous Alpha, Max's uncle, and other issues, they still had a few deeply knowledgeable elders that he hoped would be an asset at the meeting.

Max went downstairs to the kitchen to start on the coffee and see what he could make for breakfast. He knew Cheyenne liked coffee since he'd seen her drink it more than once before with a gleam in her eyes. What she wanted for breakfast, however, he didn't know. But he'd seen her eat bacon, so that would have to suffice while he waited for her to wake up so he could see how she liked her eggs—if she even liked them.

After he'd given her his shirt the night before, she'd gone to bed. He'd heard the sound of her soft breathing as she slept when he prowled by her door, his wolf—and the man—needing to know she was safe. He'd let her sleep even when Brie and Dawn brought over some clothes and things that Dhani and Kameron had collected for her. He'd ignored the joy from his wolf about the fact that Cheyenne was now drenched in his scent from his shirt. If she had waited an hour to go to sleep, that might not have been the case.

If it weren't for the fact that Kameron was mated and had literally brought his mate with him, Max might have had an issue with his cousin touching Cheyenne's things, but based on the scents, Dhani had done it all.

Max had left the suitcase near the guest bedroom door, and as he passed the room on his way to the stairs, he'd noticed the bag was inside. Cheyenne was awake. He'd have known that from the sounds of her moving around anyway, but he tried not to use his enhanced senses to spy on her.

Tried.

He heard her coming down the stairs as he placed the bacon in the oven to cook. He liked it crispy, and that was his favorite way to do it without splattering himself with hot grease. And it was easier, frankly, to move around the kitchen and work on the other parts of breakfast if he didn't have to worry about an extra pan. He missed his arm most days, but while cooking was one of the times he missed it the most. He'd learned to overcome, but he still got angry sometimes at what he'd lost thanks to the greed and fear of others.

"Good morning," he said quietly, not facing her. He

was trying to cut bread to make toast, and he needed to focus.

"Good morning." She cleared her throat. "The coffee smells amazing. May I have some?"

He nodded and looked over his shoulder, trying not to swallow his tongue at the sight of her in tight jeans and a sweater. He'd always liked her curves and had done his best not to stare at them. But since she *still* smelled of him even after her shower and she was in his house, it was hard *not* to stare.

Not to want.

Not to need.

"I made enough for us both. I remembered you liked coffee with cream, but I didn't know about the sugar. It's on the counter, though, if you need it."

She tilted her head as she studied him, the gesture so wolf that he almost forgot she was still human. He pushed away that thought though because if she were truly his mate, then she couldn't remain human for long. Her life would only be tied to his and its longevity if she were a witch or turned into a wolf. She'd eventually age and die, tearing half his soul away and losing part of herself in the process if she didn't relinquish her humanity. It wasn't an easy choice, nor was it something that had seemed fair in his mind, but they were the rules of the moon goddess from long ago, and though their deity meddled in some special cases—like theirs for instance—he didn't know what would happen when it came to Cheyenne and her humanity.

That was another discussion they'd need to have, but since he was almost forced to take her choice away once, he wouldn't do it again.

"I know we know each other and have picked up a few things over the time I've known about Dawn and her new Pack, your Pack, but I still feel like there's so much to learn. So much."

"Because there is." He shrugged and went back to cutting the bread. "Doesn't mean you have to learn it all right now."

"That's true." She worked alongside him, adding sugar and cream to her coffee. He took note of how much she used so he would be able to make it for her the next time. He didn't know why he took immense pleasure in that, but since he did, he wasn't going to push it away. He hadn't been able to find happiness or enjoyment in most things lately.

She sipped her coffee as he slid the bread into the toaster but didn't push the lever down. "Can I help?"

"I've got it down, though I don't know how you like your eggs or if you even eat bread. I know you like bacon, though."

She grinned. "I *love* bacon. The crispier, the better."

"That's my kind of bacon." He grinned at her, and his face ached as if he hadn't smiled in far too long. He didn't like to think about that.

"I like your smile," she said suddenly as if she were reading his thoughts. "You should do it more often."

His smile didn't fade, but he turned away from her. "How do you like your eggs?"

"Over-easy, but if you don't like frying them, I don't mind scrambled."

"I'm over a hundred and fifty years old, Cheyenne. I've learned how to flip an egg. And I like over-easy, too."

She stiffened next to him. "I forget that all of you are so much older than me."

He cracked the eggs in the pan and looked over at her. "We are. I'm not the youngest since the triplets—Kameron, Walker, and Brandon—have that honor, but Mitchell is my older brother."

Cheyenne stood beside him, her back resting against the edge of the counter as she sipped her coffee. "I forget that you and Mitchell aren't actually brothers with the others."

"We grew up like siblings. Our fathers were siblings and in the hierarchy of the Pack, with my Uncle Joseph being the Alpha. My dad, Abraham, was the Enforcer. They both did horrible things, along with my other uncles. They turned our Pack into something darker than what the Aspens seem like right now. The old Central Pack, the other Pack that lies between the Redwoods and the Talons, was the only one worse than us since they summoned a literal *demon* to try and take over the world. But that's another story."

Her eyes wide, she turned slightly to face him. "A demon?"

"I'll let my cousin Brynn and her mate, Finn, the Heir to the Redwood Pack, tell that story. He was only a kid when it all happened, but he was there and remembers most of it. The Centrals have a new den, a new Alpha, and a new Pack now, and when Gideon took care of our old Alpha, and we all took care of the uncles and my father, Gideon became our Alpha and the Pack slowly healed. It took decades for the moon goddess to forgive us, and for us to function like we should have been doing the whole time, but we're stronger than ever. I just wish we were stronger than the Aspens. Blade has had centuries to build up his ranks, and the man is one formidable Alpha. It's not easy to fight him when he uses powers we can't because we're not willing to risk our souls."

Cheyenne set down her coffee. "By *take care of your uncles*, you mean kill them, right? That's the only way for the hierarchy to change. For the others to die?"

He'd hoped she would miss that part of what he'd said since he'd put a lot out there just then, but he couldn't ignore it. His Pack was strong because his family made the tough decisions.

Fate hadn't allowed Cheyenne to escape that, no matter how hard she might have wanted to try. So, she would have to see the reality of where she was now, even if it wouldn't be easy for any of them.

"We killed my father and the rest because they were

killing innocents and doing things I'm not going to mention, not now, and maybe not ever. I don't like killing, but I've done it to protect my people and have done it on a battlefield."

"I get it, Max. I'm not judging. And I never would." She sounded sincere, and he figured she was.

He gave her a tight nod. "And, no, the natural way for the hierarchy to change is when the next generation is old enough, and the Alpha is ready to step down. The Redwoods moved up earlier than expected because of what happened when the demon attacked. Again, another story that's not mine to tell. My brother and cousins should have moved up about a decade or so before they did, but the old guard didn't want to relinquish control. In a healthy Pack, it would have been easy. We were not healthy. As it is, when Fallon gets older, and Brie and Gideon have a bunch more kids, those children will be part of the new hierarchy." He paused. "Well, when it's time, Ryder will give up the mantle of Heir to Fallon, and then the rest will most likely be Brie and Gideon's kids. Sometimes, it goes to cousins like it did with Mitchell. Sometimes, it goes to other members of the Pack that are needed. It all depends on the generation, and Fallon and the other kids are far too young to tell right now. Okay, other than Fallon. She already smells of a future Alpha."

Cheyenne blinked. "That's the most I've ever heard you speak."

He shrugged again, plating their meals. He was glad

that she didn't move in to help since he had it down, but he knew that if he truly needed help with something he was physically unable to do, she'd step right in. Cheyenne was good with people and with animals. He was lucky that he was both.

"You asked a question that needed a detailed answer. Want to eat in here or in the dining room?"

She took her plate and went to the kitchen island that had a couple of bar stools. "Here is fine. I love your kitchen."

The room could be hers too if their mating actually worked out.

He didn't say anything though since neither of them was ready for that.

"I like to cook. I had to change a few things around when I lost my arm, but I'm getting better at figuring out what I have to do in order to function the way I need to."

"You have almost perfect mobility, I noticed. Nothing slows you down, and it shouldn't. You just have to take a few different steps than the rest of us. I hope you know that if you need my help, though, I'll be right there. I won't barge in, but if you need me to make it easier for you, I can do it. I'm sure your family does the same since they're smart and caring people and know you need your space."

They did, and they hadn't pressed. They'd just let him do what he needed, or at least thought he needed. He'd been the one to push them away, and he was surprised at how insightful Cheyenne was about it all. Though he probably shouldn't be since she tended to study everyone and everything around her.

"We need to head to the Pack circle soon. Brie and Dawn brought over your things yesterday. And it was Dhani who picked stuff from your place, not another wolf who doesn't know you. Kameron was with her, but they said he didn't go inside since he didn't want to encroach on your space."

"Thank you for that. I'll thank them, as well. I'm doing my best to compartmentalize right now because it's so much. I already called someone to help out with the clinic and told them I'd be out for two weeks. I might lose some business, but I think it's the only way to keep them safe and for me to figure out what's going on."

"I know it sucks that we're pretty much taking over your life, but I don't really know what we can do about it right now." He wanted to reach out and hold her, to soothe her in some way, but she wasn't wolf—not yet—and it had been a while since he'd willingly touched another and let them touch him. The fact that he'd been doing so much of it with Cheyenne recently should have worried him, but his wolf wouldn't let him.

"You're not the one that stabbed me and used my blood to make some stone do something I'm not really sure I *want* to know about. You're just the one who tried to save my life."

He let out a growl, and she just sighed. "I'll kill him for that."

"You're going to have to stand in line. And not just behind me since I have a feeling that more than one of your family members wants to rip him limb from limb."

"You're not wrong."

She snorted and finished up her breakfast, him doing the same. They quickly worked on the dishes in silence—a comfortable one, thankfully—and then headed out to the Pack circle. He didn't hold her hand this time, but they were close enough that he could protect her in case something came at them. And because he wanted that free range of motion, he had his good arm away from her. Every once in a while, she brushed his other arm and the space where his lower arm and hand used to be. It should have bothered him, but it didn't, not with her.

And he had a feeling it had everything to do with the woman she was and not just because of the bond between them.

By the time they reached the Pack circle, he was aware that almost everyone was staring at the two of them. He knew that there were already rumors about Cheyenne becoming part of the Pack, even if they didn't know the full truth of it. Some of the stronger wolves would be able to feel the start of the new bonds in the Pack's magic. Others would have noticed that she'd been at the clinic with Walker rather than at a human one. And even more would have seen her walk into Max's home and come out of it the next morning. With his scent covering her thanks to his shirt the night before, some would wonder what had happened between them.

She was his mate, in bond only for now. She didn't bear his mark yet. If and when they discussed what was going on between them and what the moon goddess had done, that fact would have to change. His wolf liked the idea of her walking through the crowd with his mark on her shoulder for all to see, while the man wanted to keep what they had—or what they could have if he didn't let himself think too hard—private.

The Pack had always watched him. Once because he was the only member of his family who could smile no matter what. Max had been shielded from his father by Mitchell, he knew that. He'd gone through his own hell with his father and uncles, yes, but Mitchell had always taken the brunt of it. Max had tried to intervene, but it had never been enough. But he'd also been able to see the good in people and his Pack, the bright things in his life.

Then, everything changed, and the humans took more from him than his arm.

They took his spirit.

His will.

And then the others watched him because of that.

He slid his arm around Cheyenne, pulling her closer as they made their way to where the family would sit in the stone arena. She gave him an odd look before turning back to watch where she was going. She might not be able to feel the stares of those around them, but he could, and he didn't want anyone to think she was fair game without the mark.

She was Pack, and the bond told him that she was his.

Not that he had any idea what to do about that.

"We're letting humans into our circle now?" a wolf named Stephen asked as he blocked their path.

Max let out a warning growl. His family wasn't close enough to hear what was going on, and since he and Cheyenne were just at the right angle to be out of sight, he wasn't even sure the others knew they were near.

"Move out of the way, Stephen. We'll go over everything during the meeting."

"With her, is what you're saying." Two more wolves came closer, and though Max was more dominant than each of them, they were surrounded. Frankly, Max didn't want to show Cheyenne exactly what he could do with the strength he held in his veins.

"Yes, with me." Cheyenne lifted her chin but didn't come from behind Max where he'd subtly put his body in front of hers. She was a damn strong human, and if she chose to turn to a wolf, she'd be high on the dominance scale for sure. But she didn't have claws or fangs to fight with right now if it came to that. But she met the others' gazes, and that spoke volumes.

"She's Pack, Stephen." Max held back more of a growl since he didn't want to get into a fight in the middle of a Pack circle. "And she's mine."

He felt Cheyenne stiffen next to him, but when she slid her fingers into the belt loop of his jeans—since she couldn't hold his hand on that side of his body—his wolf prowled under his skin, wanting more.

Stephen's nostrils flared, and he lowered his gaze, as did the others on either side of him. Max knew that it wasn't just for him either, it was for Cheyenne. Stephen and the others knew who was the more dominant in this group, and it wasn't Stephen and his friends.

When they skulked off, he tugged Cheyenne toward the tree line so they could talk. He needed to get a few words out before they had to stand next to his family and deal with the world and the dangers that were greater than what was going on between the two of them.

"Well that was interesting," Cheyenne said, her brow raised. "Is that going to happen often?"

Max pinched the bridge of his nose. "It shouldn't, but like Brie said yesterday, things are off-kilter here with so many changes. Gideon and the others have a handle on it, but there are still skirmishes. And we're wolves, Cheyenne. Sometimes, our animal instincts come out to play."

"I get that. Of all humans, I get that."

She was a vet, so she would, but still... He reached out and traced his finger along her jaw, unable to hold back. His wolf wanted to do more, but he knew this wasn't the time or place.

"Thank you for defending me. Verbally, I could have

done it myself, but I know my strength and fighting skills against wolves and cats is not there yet."

"I know we need to talk about it, but I'm your mate, Cheyenne. I'm going to protect you. I would have before because you're a friend, but now it's my duty and my privilege to do so."

She licked her lips, and his gaze went to them. Unable to stop himself, he leaned forward and brushed his lips along hers. Her lips were so soft, her body so close that he could scent himself on her. She sucked in a startled breath, and he pressed forward with slightly more pressure before pulling away.

"Should I apologize for that?" he asked, his voice low. He knew they needed to go before they were late, but this was important. Everything seemed so important these days.

"No. I would have stopped you if I wanted to." She tilted her head. "I'm going to say something that's probably going to annoy you, but since we're going about this from the wrong end and, frankly, it's already worrying me, I'm just going to say it."

His wolf pushed at him, but he ignored it, worried about what she was going to say. "Okay."

"The others say you used to smile. Used to be the one who hugged and laughed and held."

He was the one who stiffened this time. "I'm not that man anymore."

She reached up and cupped his jaw. She had to go up

onto her tiptoes since she was so tiny compared to him, but he didn't move away from her touch. Didn't want to. "I know. I never knew that man. I only know the man before me. The one who isn't as broken as the world thinks."

He growled, annoyed at that word. *Broken.* "I'm not a broken man. I'm just not the same."

"I know." She pressed her lips together, staring at him as she moved her hand away. He missed the touch. "So, what does this mean?"

"I don't know, but you're stuck with me. I hope you don't mind a mate who isn't going to fucking smile." He'd used the word *mate,* and her eyes darkened. Something was going on between them, and he could feel it across the bond.

That made her smile, if only for a moment. "Whatever you say. Now, let's go see what the others say. Because it's not just about you and me. But, Max? One day, it *will* have to be you and me."

He didn't say anything, but he knew. They would do what they could for the others, fight for the Pack, and deal with this new magic. But at some point, he'd have to deal with this new mating bond tearing at the shards within him, doing what nothing could do before.

Finding him.

CHAPTER SIX

Cheyenne wrapped her fingers in Max's belt loop under his right arm once again. She liked that he trusted her enough to put that side of him toward her. She knew he didn't do it often, if ever, with others. And she knew that he had his other arm away from her so he could protect her and himself if something came at them.

She'd figure out exactly how she felt about all of it later.

For now, she found herself standing in the middle of the Brentwood area of the Pack circle, the stone seats surrounding her. The elders sat in the section next to them. She was still trying to catch up with what had just happened between her and Max, let alone what was going to happen with the rest of the Pack, as Gideon began the meeting.

Max was her mate, there was no denying that, though she didn't know what it meant in the grand scheme of things considering they had the bond but hadn't taken steps to make it happen in the first place. The kiss they'd just shared was their first true kiss, and while she could still taste him on her lips, it hadn't lasted long enough for her to sense what it meant, or what it could mean.

"You look lost," a male wolf said from her side.

She froze, then looked over at the man, his dark hair and eyes intense. And from the depth of knowledge and *time* in those eyes, she knew this wolf was far older than anyone else in this stone circle. This man, this wolf, had to be an elder.

"I feel lost," she answered, surprised she'd spoken at all.

"I'm Xavier. And you're Cheyenne, our new Packmate and Max's mate."

She blinked and held out her hand, wondering how Pack members greeted one another. She supposed sniffing each other like true wolves wasn't appropriate, plus, she wasn't a wolf.

Yet.

No, she wasn't going to think about that.

"Nice to meet you."

Xavier wrapped his hand around hers, and she swallowed hard at the power radiating from him. Oh, Max and Gideon—and probably the rest of the Brentwoods—were stronger in terms of dominance, but the saying that knowledge was power wasn't lost on this man. Or her.

"We'll speak soon, I'm sure." Then, Xavier released her hand and turned to where Gideon stood.

Though the circle was filled with the magic of the wolves, witches, and Aimee, their sole cat shifter, Gideon spoke into a microphone, probably because the Pack was so large that bellowing would get annoying after a while. He stood in front of a stone wall that held large screens where his face was shown like he was a singer at a concert or a preacher at one of those megachurches her parents used to go to until they passed when she was in college.

The arena they were in was actually outdoors, and she assumed it was because shifters were far more in tune with nature than most humans. It actually reminded her a bit of the Coliseum of ancient Rome, though far smaller and more modern with upgrades. She knew, though, that the stones she now sat on were older than she was, probably even older than Max since the Pack who created them was the first Pack to *ever* form. She hadn't known until recently, but apparently, the Talon line came from the original hunter and the moon goddess from ages ago and had evolved into what the Pack was today. Cheyenne couldn't comprehend the vast layers of history that must live within the wolves and walls of this den, but then again, maybe those who lived it didn't dwell on it. It would be hard to remember every instance of being when you lived for hundreds of years.

And she knew if she so chose, that would be her burden, as well.

She swallowed hard, and Max shifted closer, giving her strength so she could focus on Gideon as he spoke. She didn't want to think about the fact that Max soothed her as much as he did, but then again, she couldn't help but think of the man that pulsated in her chest thanks to their new bond that tasted of heat and raw power.

"Let the circle begin," Gideon bellowed into the microphone. Maybe he did need to shout after all, since speaking over hundreds of wolves at once would be difficult in any situation. She knew that not all of the Pack was there since some had to watch the younger ones and others were on patrol and guarding the den, but almost all of the Pack had to be in attendance. That meant the amount of magic and power within these stones was so immense, she could taste it on her tongue, feel it on her skin, and she wasn't even a magic user or shifter like the rest of the people surrounding her.

As soon as Gideon spoke, the wolves grew quiet. So silent, Cheyenne had to open her mouth and crack her jaw a bit since the lack of sound had almost created a vacuum that made her want to pop her ears. She couldn't explain it any other way, and when Max looked over at her, raising a brow, she shrugged. She wasn't like anyone else here, and she would just have to learn her way ...or run like she had before.

Only she didn't know if she was going to be able to run

this time, not with the new bonds settling into her without her even knowing.

"As you know, Blade has declared himself Supreme Alpha. We have no idea what he means by that, but we *do* know that something is coming from him and the Aspens."

The others grumbled, speaking to one another, and Gideon let them have that time. She figured that with so much tension in the area, having an outlet, even just a vicious whisper, would help.

"No one has ever been a Supreme Alpha or Alpha of all the wolves. That, at least, is what we think he means. He wants to rule over all the Packs, have every Alpha answer to him. And in this new world where we must live within the human rules and find our way when the world knows who we are, maybe the idea of having one governing body is a good idea."

The others growled at that and, frankly, Cheyenne wanted to, as well. She knew that having so many Packs around the world who didn't do things exactly the same way could be an issue. Some were still in hiding, others, like the Talons, had been forced out into the open. Everyone knew who the Talons were and who many of the individual wolves within the Pack were. It had been dangerous in the beginning and, frankly, Cheyenne wasn't sure it was any less dangerous now. Considering the fact that she couldn't go home at the moment because of her connections to the Packs, she just didn't know.

"Blade, however, is not our Supreme Alpha."

The others cheered, though she noticed that the Brentwoods and elders stayed silent. They all knew what was coming, after all, or at least knew what dangers they were all facing.

"One day, when we finish with the Aspen Pack, when Blade is no longer a danger to our way of life and our pups, then we will need to discuss with the other Packs a better truce." He held up his hands to stop any murmuring. And because he was Alpha, not a single person objected. Well, because he was Alpha and because he was Gideon. "Parker, the Voice of the Wolves, and now a Talon Pack member, has connected us all, something we've needed to do for far too long. We're in an alliance with the Redwoods and the Centrals, and one with a European Pack is in the works. That much you all know. It has helped us. We have grown stronger. And with what Blade most likely has in store for us, we might have to find more strength, more members of other Packs who are willing to fight alongside us. Blade has used dark magic in the past, he has threatened us over and over again, and we have always come out on top because we fought together. We must keep fighting as one. We must keep calm and find a way to remove Blade from his position. One he made up, but something that we might need in the future. Blade is not our Supreme Alpha."

The others started asking questions, and Gideon and the others in the hierarchy answered them. Cheyenne noticed that Max remained silent, part of the Brentwoods and the Pack but just separate enough because he had no true titled position. She had heard that he was part of the Talon and Redwood Pack Joint Council, but as the two Packs were practically one at this point with two Alphas, she wasn't sure what he did now or how he felt about it all. This wasn't the time or place to discuss it, however.

"As for the other business we need to settle, we're here with a plea for you all to look into your memories and help us with details." Gideon looked over at Cheyenne, and she straightened in her seat. She didn't meet his gaze, had never truly been able to, but she did look at the tightness of his jaw. Max leaned into her, and she could breathe again, unaware she hadn't been able to before.

"Blade took a friend of our Pack, one who is now Pack herself." The others growled for her, and for some reason, Cheyenne felt *protected*. These wolves—not all of them she guessed, thinking of Stephen—were on her side, at least that's how it felt at the moment. It might change in an instant, but she wasn't alone anymore.

She had her friends. She had a Pack. She had a group of people who might not be like her but were connected to her in some way. Other than Dhani, Aimee, and Dawn, Cheyenne had never truly had that in her life. Not in school or even at her clinic.

An overwhelming sense of change washed over her, and it was all she could do not to sink into Max's side and hide from the concern and awareness surrounding her.

Gideon spoke again, this time describing the artifact and what had happened to her. He didn't mention the torture, the fear she had that she could have died, or that Blade would have reveled in it. Instead, he only spoke of the artifact itself and the fact that she'd seen it.

"If you have seen this before or have read about it, tell us. Go to your homes, to your libraries, search for it. It's important to Blade. Therefore, it has to be important to us. When we convene again, we will discuss it more, but know we *will* fight Blade. We will win. And we will live in peace. It's time for our Packs to do so. Far past time."

Then the wolves in human form threw back their heads and howled. Max joined in next to her, and she shivered but didn't move away. Instead, she closed her eyes and let it all wash over her, let the magic and the sense of almost belonging seep into her soul.

When she opened her eyes, the rest of the Pack was filing out of the circle in waves, while some lingered, presumably speaking to one another about what had just happened. The Brentwoods were all talking to one another, her friends giving her reassuring glances as she sat next to Max in silence, not sure what to do next.

Xavier cleared his throat, and she looked over at him. At her side, she could feel Max doing the same.

"Yes?" she asked, a little unnerved by this wolf who seemed to know everything, to *see* everything. Yet he wasn't fully immersed in this world. He was far too old for that.

"Gideon came to me last night, came to all the elders. He spoke about what happened to you and gave more details." She winced, and Max put his arm around her while Xavier had the grace to look ashamed. "I'm sorry he had to tell us, though he might have to tell the rest of the Pack. The details of the blood and sacrifice are what triggered a memory for me."

She leaned forward and could tell others were doing the same. "And?"

She knew she sounded rude, but she also knew the Pack needed to know what was going on. *She* needed to know what was going on.

"The artifact, if it's the same one I'm thinking of, was meant for blessings. So, in times of need, if there was a disaster and they lost an Alpha, it was used to help the Pack live and thrive until the Heir could be Alpha. For instance, if Ryder and Gideon were both lost to us, Fallon wouldn't be old enough to be Alpha, and we have no Heir after her. If we had the artifact, the power could be drawn from the moon goddess herself to help settle the Pack until we were ready. Until Fallon was ready. But that's only what I read long ago. There could be other stones that look like the one you described, but I doubt there can be two stones of such power."

Cheyenne let out the breath she'd been holding, but Gideon was the one who spoke. "Why did Blade need to use it, then? His Heir is still alive, though we don't hear from him. Audrey said he was on her side though before we lost contact with her."

"Then there might be other uses for the artifact," Xavier said simply, though his words and their meaning were anything but simple.

"If it gives power, then maybe it can take it away," Max said softly, and the others froze. Cheyenne rubbed his knee when he stopped talking and, for some reason, she knew he didn't like the attention on him. "If the moon goddess is the one who gave the power to the artifact to help the Packs, then that means that power can be put *into* it. And if Blade used a blood sacrifice—"

"Then he could be using it for something it wasn't intended for," Cheyenne finished for him.

"Could he take power away from other Packs?" Gideon asked. "Because fuck us if he can. We need to tell Kade, Cole, and the others."

Kade was the Alpha of the Redwoods. Cole, the Alpha of the Centrals.

"I don't know if that's right or not," Max put in. "But making sure they know our theories could help."

Gideon gave a tight nod, then froze, his body going stick-straight, his eyes wide. Then Brie let out a scream as she fell into Mitchell's arms since he was the one closest to her. Gideon threw back his head and howled so painfully that Cheyenne thought she might die right then along with the rest of the world. Gideon clawed at his chest as the rest of the family either went into protective battle stances; or in Walker's and Leah's cases, ran to Gideon and Brie to see how they could help.

Gideon dropped to his knees, and the other wolves that weren't family fell as well, their pained howls an echo of their Alpha's.

Gideon looked at all of them, his wolf in his eyes, but Cheyenne knew something was wrong.

She could *meet* his eyes. That couldn't be right. He was an *Alpha*. She wasn't supposed to be able to meet his gaze.

"He took it," Gideon rasped. "He took my power."

Blade had done it.

He'd changed the game.

And he'd done it right as they talked about it, meaning...Blade knew.

He could see.

He could feel.

And he'd done the unthinkable.

He'd taken their Alpha.

And then Cheyenne screamed.

CHAPTER SEVEN

Max had no idea what was happening, but as soon as Cheyenne screamed, he turned to her, pulling her close. She shook, her hands going to her head as she clawed at her temples, then her chest. If her nails weren't so short, she'd have been bleeding right then, and Max couldn't do anything but try to hold her down as she screamed in pain.

Brie was no longer screaming. Instead, she was holding her mate close as Gideon tried to form words.

None of them could speak. They couldn't do anything except watch as their Alpha looked at them with the eyes of a wolf but without power. It was unthinkable. Cheyenne stopped screaming in Max's hold, her body shaking violently, her teeth chattering. He picked her up, cradling her to his chest as he tried to figure out what to do next.

Ryder looked at all of them, his hands over his heart as his mouth moved and nothing came out.

Everyone just stood there, dumbfounded, and Max didn't blame them, but they couldn't keep doing that if they wanted to survive this.

"Ryder? Do you have all the Pack bonds?" Max barked out the words, bringing everyone out of their stupor even though he hated the words themselves.

"Only as Heir. I don't feel any different." Ryder looked at the others. "Any of you?"

"The same Enforcer bonds as always," Kameron put in.

"Same for me as Beta," Mitchell added.

"Yes, as Healer." Walker sat in front of Max and Cheyenne, trying to get close, but Cheyenne couldn't handle the touch. He'd never seen his cousin look so lost before, not even during the terror of almost losing Aimee.

Nothing made sense.

"And for me as Omega." Brandon held his two mates, Avery and Parker, close. Parker was on the phone with his family, who happened to be Redwoods. Max knew he was keeping the other Pack informed.

Good, since the Talons might not be able to handle this on their own.

"So...many...bonds..." Cheyenne bit out the words, and everyone froze, looking down at her.

"Holy fuck," Max growled. It couldn't be. She couldn't be the Alpha. That wasn't how this worked.

"If Blade used the artifact to take away power, then her

blood might be connected to it. After all, he said her blood, her *sacrifice* would be the one to activate it." Xavier knelt beside Walker to try and help, but Cheyenne just burrowed deeper against Max's chest.

"She doesn't smell of Alpha, just *power*," Max said through gritted teeth. "She smells of human and *mine*. What the fuck is going on?"

Before anyone could answer, Blade was on the screen in the Pack circle, and Max knew the worst was only beginning.

"Fuck this," Max whispered, pulling Cheyenne closer to him. He had no idea what was going on, but he knew it couldn't be good.

Kameron started barking out orders to his men and women, Mitchell doing the same with his team. Max knew that soon their borders would be far more protected, the teams moving out and filling any holes or pockets that opened up. The Redwoods would be on alert, same with the Centrals.

"You didn't listen when I said I was the Supreme Alpha, and now you're facing the consequences."

Max tried not to growl. He tried not to think about what Blade was going to say next. All he could do was focus on his mate and wonder what the Alpha of the Aspen Pack was going on about.

Cheyenne still scented of power, and it worried him. Gideon still lay on the ground with Walker standing over him. His cousin didn't smell of Alpha anymore, and he had no idea what might happen next, or what they would do about it when Blade was finished talking and the world stopped falling down around them.

"You should've listened to me. But you didn't. And now, because of that, you won't have an Alpha anymore."

Max stiffened, wondering what the hell Blade was going to do because there was no way this bastard was done.

"It's only temporary. I am the Supreme Alpha. I am the one with power. And when I feel like it's time for you to have your power as Alpha back, you'll have it back. Because I am the one who's going to have the say. The power. And the will."

Max let out a growl that echoed throughout the circle, mixing with the other growls from his Pack mates. Blade was a dead man, and he didn't even know it yet. But what Max did notice was that Blade did not look healthy. The man looked grey, and sweat poured down his face. Whatever power it took for Blade to use the artifact, it had taken something from him. Max didn't know what, but he would do everything in his power to exploit that fact.

Cheyenne moaned again in Max's hold, and he pulled her closer, hoping to hell that he could find a way to fix this. Only he wasn't the kind of man that could do that anymore. He didn't have the strength needed to protect his Pack, his family, and his mate.

But he didn't have time to worry about himself right then because Blade wasn't finished.

The Aspen Alpha lifted a lip in a snarl before speaking again. "If you don't bow to my will and understand that I am the one who's going to make all the decisions when it comes to the humans, the witches, and anyone that thinks they can harm shifters, I'll make sure your precious Gideon loses his power again. That is if I give it back at all."

The others began to circle around, finally coming out of their stupor after seeing what had happened to their Alpha. Cheyenne wasn't shaking as badly as she had been, and her temperature was coming up. That was how Max noticed that she had gone icy-cold. He held her closer, knowing that his body temperature was higher than a human's because of his wolf. She snuggled into him, even as she opened her eyes, the fear in the depths bright and jarring.

Cheyenne never looked scared. Even when she had been bloody and beaten, she hadn't looked scared. But right now, her fear was *his* fear.

And the fact that he could sense it across the bond freaked him the hell out.

Blade continued talking, but Max knew it was just so the other man could hear himself speak. Blade wanted all of the power. He wanted to be the one to control humans, shifters, witches, and everything in between. Because Max knew there was more to the world than just what he could see. After all, his Pack had recently discovered that there were more shifters in the world than wolves. And he had lived a long time to just be finding that out now.

Blade finally looked around, and that's when Max figured out that Blade couldn't see the circle like Max could see Blade. The Alpha was just recording what he wanted to say and doing it live. This wasn't a two-way conversation. The other man had somehow hacked into the Talon den's system, but that was all he could do. This wasn't magic. This was technology, something that any hacker could pull off.

And Max knew his cousins would never allow this to happen again.

Blade lifted up the artifact, and Max made sure he committed everything about it to memory. And while he knew that several people were recording what was going on, and the system itself would do that, Max wanted to make sure he knew exactly what Blade was holding. Because that artifact was what was hurting his cousin, his Alpha, and his mate right then.

Blade closed his eyes, and sweat poured down the Alpha's face. Max hoped to hell that the guy would just die from using too much energy, but today wasn't going to be that day.

Gideon threw back his head and screamed. Brie did the same. But Gideon practically glowed as he stood up, his shoulders strong, and the scent of Alpha surrounding him once more. Cheyenne finally stopped shaking, the scent that had scared him and marked her as a new power now gone.

This had only been a test, but Max knew it wasn't over.

"I know you can't hear me, Blade, but I'm coming for you. You're a dead man." Gideon growled out the words, even as he stalked towards his mate and held Brie close to him. He might be holding her, but she was holding him right back. They had never looked stronger, even in the face of near defeat.

They were the Alpha pair, and Max never wanted that responsibility on his shoulders.

He might not have a title, might not be part of the hierarchy, but he was glad. He did not want that struggle, that power.

He kissed the top of Cheyenne's head and helped her to her feet. "You okay?"

"I guess. What the hell just happened?" Her hands were clammy, and he held them both in his one palm, using his other arm to bring her closer. His family was still on alert, and so was he for that matter. He kept his attention on the screen as well as anything else that could come at them while they were distracted by what was going on.

"I don't know, but I think we were right somewhat in what the artifact does."

Cheyenne moved around so she faced Gideon as well as Blade's image, but she leaned into Max, her back to his front. He didn't know if she was even aware that she was doing it, but he let it happen. They hadn't touched much except for on the battlefield at Blade's old cabin, but ever since the bond had been placed between them, they couldn't help but touch each other.

Blade sneered down at them, and Max knew he wasn't going to like anything that happened next. The air around them sizzled, and he took a deep breath, trying to engage all his senses so he could figure out what might come, what could attack.

Then, two submissive wolves, both decently young and male, were tugged into the center of the circle. They weren't pulled by another person or even by ropes. Instead, they looked like marionette dolls without the strings, an unseen force pulling them in, the fear on their eyes drenching the landscape. The fact that they were submissive hurt Max's soul far more than any other sight he could have seen.

They should have been protected.

No matter what.

Cheyenne sucked in a breath, and Max wrapped his arm around her, pulling her closer. Others began to move closer to the two wolves, who now had sweat drenching their bodies. But Max knew they would be too late.

He looked up at Blade on the screen and noticed that, once again, the man looked grey, sweaty, even paler. It would be fitting if the other man died, using too much of a power he didn't understand. But that was not how things worked. The good didn't win these days, it seemed, only those who drenched themselves in evil and pretended they were a power they had no idea how to comprehend.

And as each wolf looked at each other and then over at Max and his family, they screamed, the raw pain in their voices so intense, Max's own wolf wanted to howl back. He and his family were on their feet, running towards the pair in the next breath.

Max knew it could be a trap, but submissive wolves were supposed to be treasured. They should be loved and taken care of. They had their rank in the Pack not because they were weak, but because their strength was in things other than claws and fangs. Even Brie was a submissive wolf, and she was cherished above all others as the Alpha's mate.

Cheyenne and Max somehow reached the two wolves before the rest of them. And yet he knew it was for a reason, a purpose he didn't understand. But from the way Cheyenne practically glowed in front of him, he knew that she was connected to whatever was happening. She might not understand why, none of them did, but it was for a reason. He met her eyes, then looked over at their Alpha and prayed to the moon goddess that there would be absolution.

Absolution that didn't end in death.

But as he held one man close to him, and Cheyenne fell to her knees and put the other man's head in her lap, he knew his wishes and prayers wouldn't be answered. They never were. One man, Tony, the guy Max held, looked up, the fear in his expression so potent that Max could taste it on his tongue. All he could do was hold him and wonder why there would be such a power in the world that could do this to another from far away. Battles were supposed to be waged on the field.

They should be fought with blood, fang, and claw. They weren't supposed to happen far away, where the combatants didn't have to deal with the raw power and pain that came from torture and death. But Blade had no honor, he never had. He had run away with his tail between his legs when he was outnumbered, and now he had found something and used Cheyenne to control it. And it appeared that *something* might kill them all. Unless they figured out a way to stop the Aspen Alpha.

Max went to his knees beside Cheyenne, and while Walker and the rest of the Brentwoods surrounded them, trying to help, Max knew it was too late. And so did the two wolves in their arms. They screamed once more, and then there was silence. Just the breathing of those who'd watched two perfectly sweet and caring wolves die because they were the weakest in power for Blade to attack. Or maybe it was just because Blade had touched them in the past—touched them with his power, with his soul. Not that Blade had a soul.

Gideon let out a howl of rage, and the others echoed, the song of their pain and horror a haunting melody that Max knew he would hear in his dreams. If he ever slept again. He looked down at Cheyenne, who blinked up at him, tears streaming down her face, but she couldn't speak. He knew that because she opened her mouth, and nothing came out. Instead, she ran her hands through the man's hair on her lap, and Max knew that this was the moment everything changed. Or at least a moment that something would change.

Everything had seemed like moment after moment recently, and Max knew that things had to change if they were to survive.

Before he could think any more about that, Blade began to speak again.

Kameron and the others had already run off, most likely to check the homes of every other wolf who hadn't come to the circle. Someone else had run off to go check on the children, others to check the patrols. Just because they'd only seen two lives lost just then, didn't mean there wouldn't be more.

And as Max thought the word *only*, he was afraid that it was just the beginning.

It was always just the beginning.

"You see what I can do. You can see it clearly because I bet they're in your arms right now, soulless husks. They never should have been part of the Pack anyway. They were fodder. And they always would have been. But if the other Alphas, including your Alpha, your dear Gideon, do not recognize me as the Supreme Alpha, I will kill more. I will kill your Pack, and I will even kill those Aspens who do not fall in line with me. I will kill so many. I will take their lives, and I will not regret it. You will be the ones who regret it."

Gideon growled, and Max joined him. Even Cheyenne let out a snarl of her own, one much more human but just as fierce.

Blade began again. "So, talk to your precious Alphas, use that network your Voice of the Wolves figured out. Use that and find a way to come together and be the submissive bitches that you are. Because if you do not toe the line, I'll kill the rest. And know that I have wolves within my own den that I can start with. And I will make sure the humans know it was your fault. And then they will turn on you again, and everything will be as it should be."

Max reached out and gripped Cheyenne's hand, not knowing what else to do. He needed her touch. His wolf needed her touch. And he didn't know why he craved it so much. But as soon as his skin made contact with hers, his heart slowed just enough that he could breathe again, so he could think.

Blade wasn't finished, however. "If you kill me, if you try to come at me, you will kill all of the innocents. Because I am now connected to everything and everyone. I am the Supreme Alpha. And you will understand what this means soon."

And then, Blade was gone, and Max's Pack mourned.

But Blade had made a mistake. He hadn't come at just the Alpha, something that Max knew his family would have to talk about in detail later. No, Blade had come after those who needed to be the most cared for. He had come at those who seemed the weakest. The ones who had the most strength inside. Their deaths would light a fire within them.

They had already lit a fire within Max, and from the way Cheyenne looked ready to kill anything in her path, even without claws or a weapon, he knew that Blade had lit a fire within her, as well.

They would have to figure out exactly what had happened, why Gideon had lost his powers, and why they had come back so quickly. And not just because of the artifact itself. They needed to figure out why Cheyenne had scented of power but hadn't been Alpha. They needed to figure it all out. But first, they would mourn.

And then, they would fight.

BLADE

Blade clicked off the screen and nodded at the others in the room, including his second in command. The second in command he should have had instead of the ill-fated Audrey.

He gave his men orders to stay alert and to get the next part of their plan situated before he stood up from his chair and made his way to his personal office. He'd done the video feed in the media room they'd built for him since he needed the best lighting to make sure he got his work done.

Now, though, he needed some space.

He didn't even have the energy to visit his special project in the basement anymore. Even if he missed her screams.

As soon as he closed the door behind him, he slunk down the wall next to it, his ass hitting the floor with a pang as he tried to calm his breathing. He looked down at the stone gripped in his fist, his arm shaking, and held back a growl.

He couldn't let his men see him like this, couldn't let them hear him when he was in pain.

This damn artifact took too much power. The only reason he was still standing was because he'd taken the strength of those two wolves he'd killed in front of the Talons. Without that, he knew he'd be in far worse shape than he was.

From what he'd discovered in his research, he should have been able to thrive on the energy he'd taken from Gideon, even if he had to give it back. Using the artifact shouldn't have taken a toll on Blade at all.

It was as if something were blocking him from the power.

He was supposed to be able to siphon the energy from whoever he pointed the artifact at and take it into himself. That was what the intel said. Not that he'd done most of the research himself. Scarlett, his dead witch, and he had done some of it together, but he had outsourced the rest.

Those wolves were now dead, just like the fire witch who had gotten too close.

He refused to share the power, and that meant those who knew too much had to go.

But now he was afraid that he'd missed something, or his people had. Blade wouldn't have made a mistake, not with something of this magnitude. Someone else must have missed something.

Because whoever or whatever was blocking Blade from the true power needed to be taken care of.

He squeezed the artifact tighter.

No matter what.

CHAPTER EIGHT

Cheyenne stared down at her hands, opening and closing her fists as if she could wash away the blood. The blood that wasn't actually there because the two who had died in her and Max's arms hadn't bled.

She didn't know how her life had become this. How she could look at her hands and see blood when it wasn't there. She wasn't Lady Macbeth, or whatever classic Shakespearean play that had been from. She had never been good with those types of classes. She was a scientist, the one who looked at biology and chemistry and salivated. Trying to read books that didn't make any sense to her in a language that didn't feel like it was real had never been her favorite. She loved to read, but not stories from Shakespeare. Or were they called plays?

And now she was sitting and trying to think about

Shakespeare and plays and everything that had to do with nothing so she didn't have to think about the blood on her hands.

The blood that wasn't there.

She was a vet, had had countless animals bleed on her, some had died, others had lived. She wasn't new to the idea of death and pain. And yet seeing those men die in her arms, without a single drop of blood being shed, was almost more than she could bear.

How could Blade have done that so easily?

From what she knew of the Aspen Alpha, from what she had seen, she realized he was evil. But to take the lives of two souls so sweet and pure like he had was almost unbearable. Because even though she hadn't known those two men who died in her and Max's arms, she knew they had been precious. The bonds that tied her to the Talon Pack meant something.

They had to mean something.

She might not be a wolf, might only be newly indoctrinated into the Pack and into this idea of being connected to Max, but she knew what a submissive wolf was. She knew their worth, and what it meant to be on that dominance level of the hierarchy within the Pack. The Talons treated submissives with such love and affection and did their best to show those wolves their true worth. And the submissive wolves did the same when it came to the dominants.

Cheyenne might not know every single aspect of what

was needed to be a wolf in the Talon Pack, but she knew to treat the submissives with care and compassion.

And Blade had taken their souls, had killed them without raising a hand, except for to squeeze the stone harder.

He had done all of that without blinking.

And now, two men were dead, and Cheyenne sat on Max's couch, staring at her hands, wondering what would happen next.

Because something would happen next. It always did. There would be pain. There would be death. And there would be change.

And she needed to figure out where she would end up when it all happened.

It still wasn't fair to her that this was her life, but that wasn't the true unfairness of the situation.

What was unfair, was that she had to somehow figure out how to take the next step when it came to this Pack and the man who she knew was in the house with her but had given her space to try and figure out her thoughts.

The meeting had stopped abruptly once Blade went off-screen while they were in the Pack circle. It had actually ended before that when Gideon said to think about what the artifact could do and whether they had seen it in the past. But as soon as those two wolves died, men Cheyenne couldn't even call by name, everything had changed.

She kept saying that. That things were changing, and she would have to figure out what that meant.

And sitting here staring at the blood on her hands, the blood that wasn't really there, just meant that she was doing nothing. She was wallowing in her grief, heartache for a life she had lost, and for two men she didn't know. Grief for the peace she'd thought maybe the Talons could find even in the depths of war and frustration.

And then again, she looked down at her hands, this time only seeing the pale flesh. A physician's hands, a doctor for those in need, those who couldn't put voice to their pains and hurts.

These hands should help.

And yet they had only held death that day.

Her blood had opened up that artifact. Without her blood, without her sacrifice, maybe those men would still be alive.

"You need to stop looking down at yourself and thinking those thoughts."

Cheyenne looked up at Max as he stalked into the room, a glower on his face.

"What are you talking about?"

Max lifted a brow before leaning against the wall in front of the hallway. He was still in the living room, but he was giving her enough space so she could think. It was always hard to think when Max was around. And, honestly, it was hard to even comprehend that because it hadn't been that way before. Before the bond, before the forced mating, she had been able to be near Max and not feel like she was drowning in emotion, grief, relief, and everything in between.

"I know we're still trying to figure out who we are, but I know you, Cheyenne. I know you're blaming yourself for not being able to help those men. But none of us were able to help them. And all we can do now is mourn Tony and Jason and then fight for their sacrifice."

"I hate the idea of it being called a sacrifice. They didn't offer themselves up for it. Instead, Blade chose them for some reason. Why did he choose them?"

Max shook his head before pushing off the wall and taking a seat on the coffee table in front of her. He was so close, she could scent him. The fact that she could smell him when she knew he wasn't wearing cologne probably should have worried her. But everything was so out of focus for her right then, it wasn't as if she could really think about how things had been before between them. Or even how things were before when it came to herself.

"He chose them because he thought they were weak. They were the weakest submissives that we had, but that did not make them weak."

"I know. I see the way Brie acts around the others. And I truly see the way they react around her. She's amazing. She's submissive. And she's so strong. Those men did not deserve to die. None of the wolves in this den deserve to die, but for some reason, I feel like saying especially those men."

Max reached out and traced patterns on Cheyenne's knee. She sucked in a breath, aware that he was so close, mindful that something was changing between them, but also conscious of the fact that they needed to talk about many things, not just what was happening between them.

"Those two men had their own strengths. And Blade chose them for his own reasons. But it could've been quite simply...they were the easiest to get to. The easiest to connect with. Blade isn't part of the Talon Pack. He isn't part of anything having to do with us other than our enemy. And I think that should scare us more than anything."

Cheyenne didn't reach out and touch Max, but she did soak in his warmth. "You think that if he can connect to two wolves within the Talon Pack, as well as Gideon, he can do it to any Pack."

She hadn't asked it as a question, but Max answered anyway.

"Yes. I think the artifact allows him to do that. And I don't think it was supposed to do that. But he's tainted it, somehow bastardized it into what it is now. And I think it's only the beginning. He's going to use the weak, the innocent, in order to make Gideon do what he needs him to do. And he's going to do the same with Cole and the Central Pack, and Kade and the Redwoods. There will be nothing he can do about it. My cousin, that is. Gideon is going to hate himself. My Alpha is going to hate himself."

Cheyenne shook her head, and this time reached out

to grab Max's other arm. And because that was the arm without the lower half, he froze. It was the first time she had reached out and touched him like that, but if they were going to figure out what this new thing was between them, he would have to get used to it. *She* would have to get used to it.

"I think your brother, your cousins, and all the other Alphas, are going to stand strong. But I think we'll lose people in the end, and that scares me more than anything. I keep looking down at my hands and seeing blood that isn't there. And it scares me. Because I'm just a human, a human connected to all of this, and there's nothing I can do. Blade already tried to kill me once. He would have succeeded if it wasn't for you and the moon goddess."

"I could kill him for that. Kill him just for that. But he deserves to die for so many other things." Max growled out the words, and though that should have scared her, it didn't. It just made her feel stronger. It made the connection between them more intense.

After the Pack meeting had fizzled, others had come to take away the bodies, and Cheyenne knew their families would deal with what happened next, and the Brentwoods would help with the services. She also knew that everyone else who actually had a position and title in the Pack had a job to do. The children would be taken care of, and the rest of the Brentwoods each had a role. And, somehow, she and Max had been left out. Somehow, the two of them had been sent off alone to Max's home, to the house she was now staying at for however long, and neither of them had a job to do. That meant they had all the time in the world to think about their faults and the fact that they weren't strong enough to get anything done.

At least she felt *she* wasn't strong enough. She knew that Max was far stronger than she could ever hope to be. And probably stronger than he thought he was.

"You're thinking too hard again, and it's giving you a little line between your brows right here." Max reached out and brushed his finger down her forehead, and she reared back. He froze and looked at her with wide eyes. She hated the pain she saw there before he masked it.

So, she reached out and gripped his hand. "I'm sorry, you just startled me. You didn't do anything wrong."

"I don't know what to do when it comes to you, but then again, I don't know what to do when it comes to anyone else either." Max let out a breath. The two of them didn't touch each other, but they were close enough that she could feel the heat of him. "We're sitting here alone in my house because we don't have a job to do. I could go out on patrol, but I don't want to leave you alone."

Cheyenne scowled. "I don't need a keeper."

"I know you don't need a keeper, but I also know that this is all hard for you. And, frankly, we have to talk about the giant wolf in the room."

Cheyenne snorted. "Wolf? I thought it was an elephant."

"I prefer to think of just wolves. Or, I guess cats now that Aimee's one of them."

Cheyenne shook her head. "And by giant wolf in the room, do you mean the fact that we're mated and haven't really talked about it? Or the fact that I have no idea why I can sometimes feel what you're feeling, or at least have a really strong reaction to the fact that you must be feeling something? Because it's starting to freak me out."

Max reached out and cupped her face with his hand, surprising her.

"That would be the wolf I'm talking about."

She froze, not knowing what to do when he was so near. Then again, she never knew what to do when he was close. She hated that. Hated feeling that she was so far out of her depth that she was making mistake after mistake.

He pulled away even farther, and she tried not to miss him. He looked over her shoulder, and from the way his eyes focused on nothing, she knew he was thinking and not actually pulling away from her the way she thought he might be.

"The others are working on what they need to do in order to keep the Pack safe."

She might have thought he was changing the subject, but since her thoughts had been on a similar path as his before, she nodded.

"And you want to be with them."

He shook his head, meeting her gaze. "I'm not part of the hierarchy. Not really. I'm a council member, but that's in title only these days with our treaty with the Redwoods sealed in blood and mating at this point. I go where the others need me." He let out a breath. "And I think they need me to help with this."

"What's this?"

"You. The artifact. The connections. Because there was something there, Cheyenne."

She nodded, her hands shaking. "I know. I don't know what to think about it, but it was scary. I've never felt that way before, not even when Blade stabbed me and left me for dead."

This time, Max's growl rumbled so loudly, she could feel it in her chest.

"You and I are going to figure it out together. I know you don't like standing still, and, frankly, I don't either. So, we're going to do all the research we can on this artifact, and we're going to see how you're connected so we can make it stop. I won't lose you, Cheyenne." He paused. "Not when I just found you."

She froze again. "I...I'll help. But, Max?"

He shook his head. "I don't know why I couldn't sense you were mine, or that you *could* be mine before the moon goddess changed it all. Maybe it's because of what happened on the battlefield. Maybe it's because of every-thing else going on within the Pack, but I can feel you now, Cheyenne. I can feel you in my soul."

He placed his hand over his heart, and she swallowed hard.

"I don't know what's going to happen, Max. But this is permanent, isn't it? There's no going back, even if we aren't the ones who took the steps to begin with."

"We can try to make it easier for you," he said, his voice oddly calm. "We can separate and ease the ache between us and the bond. If you want nothing to do with this, I can make it happen. But the bond is always going to be there. I've only heard of one bond breaking, and it almost killed everyone involved, and it required dark magic to even get there at all. So, no, I can't break the bond, but I can try to stay away."

Cheyenne didn't know why she hurt like this, why she never wanted to hear those words again. She might not have chosen this, but it was her life now. She wouldn't walk away.

And when it came to Max, she wasn't sure she *could*.

So, she did the only thing she could do.

She leaned forward and kissed him.

He didn't move for a moment as if surprised, then he leaned forward and deepened the kiss. He tasted of coffee and Max, and she wanted more. Craved more.

When she pulled back to breathe, she rested her forehead on his. "There's no going back, Max."

"Then do you want to make it official?" he asked, his wolf in his voice. "We're starting from the wrong direction, but we can make this ours. Then figure out the rest along the way."

In answer, she kissed him again, taking a chance on a

fate she'd never known she wanted to take, but then again, her life up until this point hadn't been as normal as she'd thought it was either.

Max was hers, and she'd figure out what came next.

In his arms, with her mouth on his.

One breath at a time.

Max cupped her face, and she went to her toes, wanting more, wanting his mouth. This wasn't about walking away from him and what could be. This was about walking toward it.

"You taste like bliss," he whispered, and she moaned. Then he moved his hand down to her side before reaching around to lift her off her feet. She immediately wrapped her legs around his waist, keeping her mouth on his.

He carried her to the bedroom and set her on the edge of the bed. He hovered over her, his lips soft and gentle as they explored each other with kisses.

"Are you sure?" he asked, his voice a shuddering whisper that sent shivers down her spine.

"I'm sure."

Then, they were taking off their clothes, pulling up their shirts, and slowly working together until he stood before her completely naked and bare. He was so beautiful —lean muscle that begged for her hands.

She couldn't help but lower her gaze to below his waist, her eyes widening. He was long, thick, and growing before her eyes.

She swallowed hard and, before she could wonder if he

would actually fit, he moved forward and kissed her again. This time, his hand gently cupped her breast and plucked at her nipple.

His tongue worked magic on her mouth as he moved from breast to breast, nipple to nipple. Shocks of sensation covered her body, and she writhed on the edge of the bed, spreading her legs wider. He moved closer to her, his cock hard and firm against her wet heat. But he didn't press, didn't move more than to keep kissing her.

Then, before she could beg for him to be inside her, he went to his knees.

She gasped as he put his mouth on her, licking and sucking at her pussy. He put both of her legs on his shoulders and kept licking, kept sucking. When he worked his fingers inside her, she moaned his name, arching herself closer to his face as her body shook.

This man knew how to eat a woman out and knew exactly what to do to get her ready.

So, it was no surprise that she came hard and kept coming as he continued to lick. Before she could beg him to stop or keep going, he was standing again, and his mouth was on hers. She could taste herself on him, and it only made her writhe more.

She moved back when she couldn't handle it anymore and reached between them, her hand encircling his hard cock.

"Cheyenne," he groaned. "I can't last if you touch me. Not this time."

"Then get inside me."

He licked his lips, then looked at her. "You know we can't use a condom. Because I need to spill my seed inside you to complete the bond. I don't have any diseases and can't catch them as a wolf. And it's not the right time to get you pregnant, at least for wolves and the phases of the moon. Okay? I have to go in bare. And then I have to bite you to mark you. It won't hurt, not with how I'll do it. I promise it's not going to hurt."

She nodded. "I know. I trust you."

Heat flashed in his eyes, and he moved over her, kissing up her body before taking her lips. Then, he was right at her entrance, but he pulled back slightly to look into her eyes.

"Yes, Max. Just the two of us. Now."

"As you wish, mate of mine."

They both sucked in ragged breaths as he entered her, his thickness stretching her almost to the point of pain. But he went so slowly, was so careful with the way he gently thrust in and out of her to make sure she could accommodate him, that it didn't hurt.

Nothing hurt with him.

Not in this moment.

Then he was inside her fully, and they were both moving, clinging to each other as if they never wanted to let go. And when she was close, and she knew he was as well, she turned her head to the side, baring her shoulder.

Max's fangs elongated, but she didn't feel scared.

Instead, a sense of purpose and becoming washed over her. When he slid his fangs into her shoulder, she realized he'd been right. It didn't hurt.

Instead, it made her come on his cock right then and there.

She screamed for him as she came, and he filled her, warm and full, almost hot.

The thread between them flared, cementing the bond even more than she thought possible.

He was her mate in truth.

Her mate forever.

There was no going back.

There never had been.

CHAPTER NINE

Max woke up far too early the next day, knowing he had studying to do and meetings to attend, but he also knew that he wasn't about to get out of bed anytime soon. Not with Cheyenne sprawled on top of him, her naked body plastered to his.

They were mated in truth.

Their bond was stronger than it had been before.

And, for some reason, she'd taken a chance on him.

Cheyenne shifted in her sleep, and he pulled her in just a little bit more. He knew they needed to get up, both of them had more than a few things to get done that day, but Max needed this moment—and he figured she did, too.

She might not be awake just yet, but given that she was lying peacefully in his hold, he figured this was something she needed. She hadn't been able to rest recently. Everything around them had changed to the point where they were running quickly, the candle burning at both ends, and just this moment, this bit of peace, might be the best thing for both of them.

Max let her sleep for another thirty minutes, and when she rolled over and stretched, he shifted as well, looking down at her. He didn't smile, wasn't sure he had enough of that in him just yet, but he did lean down and brush his lips over hers. She smiled lazily up at him before the meaning of exactly what they had done washed over them.

They were mates. There was no going back from that. Yes, the moon goddess had altered their fate and made it so this was how they would live. But the night before, both of them had chosen their own paths.

And she was the one who had taken the first step.

Maybe he should have been the one to do it, but the fact that his mate was strong enough to do it on her own and tell him exactly what she wanted—and, frankly, what they both needed—told him that maybe the moon goddess had actually chosen well.

He shouldn't have even used the word *actually*. Because, given his cousins and brother with their mates, the moon goddess knew what she was doing.

Though he would love to know what his deity was thinking right now, considering that he and Cheyenne had been mated before they'd even made that choice.

"Why are you looking at me like that?" Cheyenne looked so sleepy and sexy that it was hard for him to not want her again, even though this moment wasn't for that. He didn't deserve her, but damn if he would let her go.

Max shook his head, pulling himself out of his thoughts. "I'm just looking at you."

"And you're having some pretty serious thoughts as you do. But, then again, I guess everything we do is pretty serious these days."

Max leaned on his arm and used his left hand to brush her hair from her face. He loved rolling the honey-colored strands through his fingers. Sometimes, her hair looked darker, other times, a little lighter. He never knew exactly what color her hair was since it depended on the light she was in. Max had spent months trying not to look at her, trying not to notice her. Because she hadn't been his mate.

At least, that's what he'd thought.

But between the connections to the Pack and his own relationship with his wolf, he hadn't been able to sense who she was to him. And maybe fate had changed completely when the moon goddess made her decision. Maybe Cheyenne hadn't been meant for him at first. But there was no way he was letting her go now. If he could figure out the words to say, he'd actually tell her that.

"Can I ask you a question?" Cheyenne reached up and brushed her fingers along his jaw. He nodded.

"Of course. I bet you have a lot of questions."

"And I hope I have many years to figure out all those answers, but my question is actually about the bond. Does it feel stronger? Or is it just me?"

"I was just thinking that while you were sleeping. The bond we had before, it was there, we could both feel it, but now? Now, it's different."

"Because we both chose it. And I know we need to talk about what's happening, and what the future means, but right now, I think we're okay. And I think we're just going to have to figure it all out. Because running away from fate before didn't help me, and I'm done trying to wait for the calm and analytical parts to work out. I spent forever it seems, trying to make sure I fit the mold of who I needed to be, trying to make sure my brain worked exactly the way it needed to. And then, as I watched my friends drop one by one and fall in love and mate into this Pack, my brain decided that, okay, it's time for me to walk away."

Max held back a growl, not wanting to think about the fact that if Blade hadn't taken Cheyenne, Max might not have her in his life. But that was far too selfish of a thought for him to even think, so he wasn't going to say it out loud. But from the look in her eye, he had a feeling she knew exactly what he was thinking anyway. And that scared him.

"I don't think you would've left completely. I don't think your friends would have let you do that."

"I'm a little more stubborn than they think I am. And, honestly, I didn't want them to watch me age and fade away. And I know that I'm going to have to change into a wolf, Max. I know that a human mating into the Pack doesn't work out. And because I'm not a witch like some of the others, I'm going to have to change. I know that. And it's scary. Because I know not everyone survives. But that's something we can think about later. Maybe after we figure out exactly what this artifact is and what Blade's final plans are for it. Because I never want to watch someone die like that again, Max. I never want to watch Gideon fall to his knees and scream because of the pain of losing all his power. And I never want to feel it in my veins again. I'm not supposed to have that kind of power, Max. I'm not supposed to have anything like that. I'm human. Even if now I'm mated to a wolf."

Max leaned forward and brushed his lips along hers, the tremble of her voice bringing his wolf to the forefront. His other half pawed at him, but Max just held it back, knowing that he would soon show her his wolf, and she would be one, as well. But she was right. First, they needed to figure out the end of the world.

The end of their world, at least.

"Max? We're going to do this together. The rest of the Pack each has their own duties, and you and I are going to figure out exactly what Blade is doing. And we're going to end him. Because this was personal before, but now, it's painfully so."

And from those words alone, Max knew that he could love Cheyenne. He'd truly thought he would be alone until the end of his days. He had believed the moon goddess blessed him with life after his near-death experience. The fact that he had lost part of himself physically, and even part of his connection to his wolf had somehow put the thought into his brain that this, mating, wasn't for him.

He would always be the lone man standing on the side, watching the others live. Because living for him after everything that had happened wasn't the same as it was for everyone else. He always felt like he was on borrowed time, *stolen* time. And having a mate never made sense.

But the moon goddess had once again changed everything for him. And now, he was going to have to figure out how to live with that.

"We need to go to the meeting. And we'll make sure that everyone knows we're here to help. That we're here to figure out what the hell is going on."

Cheyenne rose on tiptoes and kissed his jaw, and his wolf howled while the man shivered. He could lose himself in her touch, become intoxicated with the idea that she was his forever. And maybe that should scare him more than it did, but he wasn't scared. Because the rest of the world was falling apart around them, and believing in something other than himself might just help him save everything.

Or at least save himself.

THE FIRST TIME Max had sat in this building, he'd found himself part of the Talon and Redwood Pack Joint Council. Now, instead of using the building as a meeting place between Packs trying to find a tentative accord so they could remain not only healthy but also stave off any outsiders who wanted to harm them, they were using it to try and protect the world. Again.

Only this time, there were more than just two Packs and their leaders.

The Alphas of each of the surrounding Packs in the area, including one from far across the Atlantic, had decided to come together in person—at least with those in America—to try and figure out exactly what they were going to do with Blade. Because there was no way they could let this continue.

They had all done their best to get at the other Alpha, but it wasn't easy when Blade had his witch and the rest of his Pack using dark magic and every other putrid thing their Packs wouldn't use.

A few decades ago, when the Redwoods were battling the original Central Pack, the Centrals had summoned a demon, sacrificing some of their own daughters to bring it into the world. The Redwoods had almost lost because they hadn't been able to sacrifice their souls and part of the world to take out the demon.

It had taken not only the moon goddess, but also the Redwoods and Talons working together to bring down that demon, and the infected Central wolves who had come from that disaster.

Because once dark magic entered a Pack, the bonds frayed and decayed. The current Central wolves were only alive because the original elders, and some of the mothers and children, had been able to get away. And when they broke from the Centrals, the moon goddess had protected them. She hadn't been able to do much, but she had hidden them from view, shielded them from the old Alphas and that demon.

Now, the Centrals were stronger. They were an actual Pack again. The Redwoods were far stronger than they had been before, too, and they had been formidable back then.

Decades ago, the Talons were just coming into what they are now. When Max's uncle finally succumbed to his fate. Gideon and Mitchell had even gone to the Redwoods to help fight on that final day. It had been the start of their new alliance that was now forged in blood and bonds.

Max had wanted to go back then, but someone had to stay within the Talon den walls to ensure that their weak were safeguarded and that those who were on the old Alpha's side were weeded out.

It had taken what seemed like forever for their Pack to become who they were now.

Max just prayed they were strong enough to beat the Aspen Pack and Blade.

Because even though they had won every battle so far, the fact that Blade was still alive and coming at them, told Max that it hadn't been enough.

But it would be enough.

It had to be.

Cheyenne sat by his side, talking with Dawn as the two of them caught up. When he and Cheyenne had walked into the building together earlier, not hand in hand but with her fingers wrapped in his belt loop like she was prone to do now, the others had all turned. He secretly loved that Cheyenne did that. He needed it. They couldn't hold hands, but they had their own version.

But when they walked into the building, everyone had looked at them. Cheyenne bore his mark, and he wore her scent. It wasn't just a bond that only some would notice because that was what they were in-tune with. Now, it was true. And while some looked surprised that it had moved so quickly, others just smiled—perhaps thinking that some light in this darkness was worth it.

And maybe he was already falling for her because of her strength. Maybe, if he were lucky enough, she could fall for him, too.

But he wasn't going to think about that right then.

Each of those in the hierarchy and the center family had been invited to this meeting. And considering that the Jamensons and the Brentwoods had a lot of siblings, there were more than a few people in the building. Not everyone had come, of course. Because the council building was situated in the middle of the Redwood and the Talon Pack lands. And that meant they were closer to the Central den than anything. However, considering that this was neutral territory, that meant everybody was safe from each other—just not the outside world.

They were hidden from the human satellites, even though the government probably knew where they were. They liked to think they knew where everyone was at all times. But that wasn't something Max was going to get into just then.

The Talons had left some of their hierarchy and their stronger wolves back in the den to protect their people. They could've had the meeting at any of the dens, even going all the way to Europe to meet the European Pack Alpha in person if they needed to. But this first meeting, where they were truly coming to terms with exactly what had to be done, needed to be held in this place that had started the treaty between the Redwoods and the Centrals and the Talons.

Max knew he and Cheyenne had just succumbed to their fates, had taken each other as true mates. They knew if they were worried about what was going on between them, their focus wouldn't be on what was going on around them. But they'd still had a moment just to themselves. That counted for something, but couldn't be the only thing between them.

Max shook himself out of his thoughts because, right then, there were three Alphas speaking in person, with the fourth on the screen above them. The Coven leader of the highest Coven in the United States was also near. That told Max the strength of magic that was located in the Pacific Northwest.

Leah had once been part of the Coven, or at least her

family was. When her brother died, Leah had become part of the Talons, and everything had shifted once again. The Coven had to be restructured. When the witches were forced to come out into the public eye just like the wolves had been, they moved to the Talons' side. And that meant, over time, their connections had grown even stronger.

Max figured having some of the strongest witches in the world as allies was a good thing.

It was Kade, the Alpha of the Redwood Pack, who began speaking. "I know I'm not the only one who felt what happened yesterday."

This wasn't surprising to Max, because his cousin, Brynn, who was now a Redwood Pack member since she was mated to the Heir of the Pack, had told them what had happened. But from the look on the European wolf's face, he hadn't expected it.

Allister, the Alpha of the Thames Pack, what Max always referred to as the European Pack, shook his head, a mix of anger and relief on his face. "It happened here, too. He killed two members of my Pack and took away my power. But then he gave it back pretty quickly. He didn't even give us a message that was just for us. It seems that he reused the message from the Talons. Apparently, over here on the other side of the Atlantic, we're not even good enough to have our own video message."

The others started growling, speaking to one another as the ramifications of exactly what had happened hit them.

"That means Blade was able to attack four Packs that we know of, all at once."

Gideon pinched the bridge of his nose as he spoke, and Brie reached out and rubbed his shoulder. In any other grouping of wolves, the fact that a submissive wolf, a mate, was there to soothe their big, bad Alpha, might have been seen as weakness. But it didn't when it came to the wolves in this room. Every single one of them had been through their own torture, their own pain, and having Brie there soothed them all. Max wasn't even sure they would've been able to meet in a room like this with so many internal dominance battles happening without someone like Brie there.

The Alpha female was a gift, and it had taken some a while to figure that out.

"I'm trying to figure out if it happened anywhere else, but for now, it seems we're the big four in Blade's eyes." Parker took notes as he spoke, and Max looked over at his cousin-in-law. Parker had once been a Redwood Pack member but had come over to the Talons when he mated the Talons' Omega, Brandon, and their other mate, Avery. Parker was the Voice of the Wolves. It was his job to go to every single Pack in the United States, and some in Europe, to figure out exactly how they were going to communicate, keep some of their secrets, and just survive in a world where technology and humanity had changed to the point where they couldn't hide anymore.

Parker's work had saved them countless times in many

ways, but it had also connected them via the system that Blade used to get at them.

Max didn't blame Parker, and he knew the others didn't either, but Parker blamed himself. Thankfully, the other man had two mates to help kick that thought out of his head.

"I know I'm new to this whole Alpha gig, but having my power stripped like that? I never want to feel that again." Cole rubbed at his chest, and his sister, Dawn, reached out and squeezed his hand. Cole didn't have a mate yet, but he had a decently strong base when it came to his hierarchy.

But the Centrals were a new Pack, a young one. The Talons and the Redwoods had taken them under their wings and were helping them navigate, but only time would make them into the Pack they wanted and needed to be. The fact that the Aspens were attacking them at all was just cruel.

Back when they were deciding if the Centrals could even be a Pack after everything that had happened, Blade had been vehemently against it. He had thrown things and loudly voiced his disapproval. He had growled and tried to make sure the Centrals were wiped from the face of the Earth. He hadn't liked the mistakes the others made, even though Blade was making even more mistakes himself.

But maybe it was more the fact that Blade hadn't liked looking into a mirror and seeing what was reflected there. Or perhaps Blade was just insane.

The other man wanted all the power, and he didn't want weakness around him.

"Has anyone heard from Audrey?" Gideon asked. "We haven't heard from her since we all figured out that cat shifters were among us. And that worries me."

Everyone shook his or her head, and Max spoke up. "I don't know if Blade would've killed her. We haven't heard about a shift in the hierarchy, even if we're not getting much information out of there at all. But if there was a new Beta, we would know. Our wolves would let us know. I don't think Audrey can get to us, but if we take out Blade, we can make sure Audrey's okay."

Cheyenne reached out and squeezed his hand. He looked over at her but didn't smile. He wasn't the smiling type. Not anymore. "We'll find her. And we're going to take out Blade. Because we can't give up."

The Alphas looked at him and nodded, respect in their eyes. Max didn't meet their gazes completely because even though he was dominant, he wasn't an Alpha. Cheyenne didn't meet their gazes either, but the fact that she had been able to during that Pack circle just told him something was going on that they truly didn't have the answers to. She'd had the strength to meet the Alpha's eyes before, but not now.

"And what are we going to do about this artifact?" Allister asked.

Cheyenne spoke up this time. "I don't think hiding the fact that I'm connected to it is going to help anyone. You all know how the artifact came into being, or at least how it was activated, and the fact that I almost died. But we all believe the moon goddess stepped in to keep me alive. And I'd like to think that while it was to keep me on this Earth and even connected to Max, maybe it was because my connection can help us. I don't know what it means, but Max and I are going to find out."

She took a deep breath before she continued, and Max leaned closer, trying to give her strength. "You all need to keep your Packs safe, and I'm not the person to do that. I don't have experience in battle strategy or even magic. But I spent many years studying, and I'm going to keep studying. So, if you'll let me, I'm going to try to help. And I will do all in my power to make sure your Packs are okay. Because I'm Pack now. I'm Max's mate. I'm a Talon. And I've always been connected to the people in this Pack, ever since I found out they existed. I don't want Blade to win. And he can't. So, I'll help in any way I can. Anything I can do. Anything."

The respect in the Alphas' eyes at that point was even stronger than it had been for Max. Max reached out and gripped her hand, his wolf practically preening like a freaking cat.

She had spoken to the Alphas, four of the strongest Packs in the world, as if she were equal to their dominance level, as if she held that strength. And Max knew she did. Just because she was human didn't make her any weaker than anyone else in the room. Oh, she might not have the same physical strength as some of the others. Or, frankly, any of the others. But emotionally and mentally? Honestly, she might be the strongest one in the room.

Maybe that was just the new mating bond speaking.

The others started talking about plans for protection and evacuation if it came to that. They all knew that, eventually, they might have to speak to the human government about what was happening, but that was a tricky subject and not something easily done.

But as the Alphas gave Cheyenne and Max permission to do their research and try to figure out if Cheyenne's connection to the artifact could help in any way, Max knew that he finally had a purpose.

It had only taken finding a mate in the most painful and unusual way for him to know where he truly stood.

At Cheyenne's side.

CHAPTER TEN

Cheyenne could barely keep her eyes open, but she didn't want to stop reading. She'd spent the past few days going over text after text with Max and some of the elders. And while learning more of the history of not only the Talon Pack but all shifters in general was invaluable, her eyes hurt, and she had to remind herself that she was indeed human and not a paranormal entity like everyone else in the den.

She might be connected to an ancient artifact and, apparently, had scented of Alpha as she screamed and writhed in pain in Max's arms, but she was still human.

At least for however long she had until she turned into a wolf. There was no way she *couldn't* take that step if she didn't want to age and die while bonded soul-to-soul with Max.

She didn't really understand why humans had to lose

their humanity in order to join a Pack. Witches were able to link their life forces with their mates' and didn't have to go through the brutal change that came from turning into a shifter.

Apparently, you had to be near death to make the change, though, and a very strong wolf—or a lion, in her best friend's case—had to be there to change the person. Max had done that for her. She had truly been near death, and he had shifted and tried to change her. She didn't remember the pain, and in retrospect, she had a feeling the moon goddess had shielded her from that. But Max had bitten her, the enzyme that turned human to shifter seeping into her skin. But it hadn't taken because of what the moon goddess later did.

If Max had succeeded, Cheyenne would be a shifter right now.

But would she be his mate?

That, she didn't know, but there was no going back now. They'd not only slept together, Max had also marked her. Their bond was stronger than ever. It was new, and Cheyenne was still trying to figure out exactly what it all meant, but she *was* figuring it out.

One moment at a time.

"We've been at this for hours, let's get home." She looked up as Max came to stand by her small desk in one of the elder's libraries. The fact that he'd said "home" and she thought of his place should have worried her, but her brain was too full for those thoughts right then.

"I could use a snack, and then bed." She stretched out her back, rolling her neck. She hadn't worked this many hours studying since she was in vet school. The fact that she was doing so now on a subject that was so unlike anything she'd ever studied before made her head hurt. But it would all be worth it. Because someone had to know something, even if it was just in the words of a long-forgotten book, or even in a memory an elder did their best to walk them through.

"I'll make sure you get something to eat, and then I'll tuck you right into bed." Max leaned over and kissed her on the forehead. She smiled up at him, even though she knew it was still a little awkward between them. They were trying to figure out not only their relationship but also where they fit within the Pack and with each other. They were not only dealing with the rest of the world and the fact that the human government might find out exactly why Cheyenne wasn't part of what she once was in her life anymore. But, soon, she would have to explain to everyone why she wasn't coming back.

Because there was no coming back from this.

She would have to face her fate and, hopefully, save the world at the same time.

She snorted, and Max gave her a weird look.

"What are you laughing at?"

"I was just trying to put what we're doing into words in my head, and it always ends with saving the world. I have no idea how it ended up like this. One day, I'm helping a litter of kittens. The next, I'm searching for an ancient artifact and exactly what it means in the grand scheme of things so we can save the world from an evil conqueror." She paused, shaking her head. "There's nothing funny about that. I know, but I can't help it. I think I'm tired. Just too tired to think clearly at this point."

Max held out his hand. "Then let's get you home." He paused. "Or, I guess, my place. Where you're staying."

Cheyenne put her hand in his and allowed him to help her out of her chair. She leaned against him, pressing her front to his as she kissed his bearded jaw. He hadn't shaved in a couple of days, and she liked the stubble.

"You can say 'home.' I was just thinking that I liked that. I know we're moving fast and, honestly, moving in a direction I never thought we'd ever take, but there's no use looking back and wondering what-if." She was the one to pause this time. "Unless we're looking back to see what was, not what couldn't be."

Max let go of her hand so he could trace her jaw with his finger.

"I like the fact I'm getting to know you. And, I like that you like the word *home*. You surprise me, Cheyenne. With every move you actually force yourself through, with every decision you make, I admire you."

Since they were standing, he only had to lean down a little bit farther to kiss her. His lips were soft, his beard just a bit scratchy, and she knew if she weren't careful, she could become addicted to him. He tasted of everything she never thought to crave.

And, she had no idea what that meant.

He gently bit her lip and then pulled back so she could put her fingers in his belt loop, and the two of them could make their way out of the elder's library and back to their place.

Okay, maybe it was still his place for now. But Cheyenne would get used to calling it home. It was odd to be able to think about the mundane things of the outside world when everything around her was pushing at her. Her heart hurt, as did everything else. It was as if everybody was at the edge of a precipice, waiting for the end to come, awaiting a change that would irrevocably alter their landscape.

Blade held all the power, and if they weren't careful, they wouldn't be strong enough to take him out. It wasn't as easy as it was in the movies with one strategic sniper strike. They couldn't get through the Aspen wards, and they couldn't start an all-out war that caused the human governments to come at them, as well. Everything was happening at such an odd and tenuous time that it was difficult to see an ending.

But, Cheyenne had to have hope. The Talons had far more faith than she ever realized. After everything they had been through, they still believed in what they were doing and in the reasons they had to do it.

If the Talons were to go to the dark side—she snorted

at that thought—and use dark magic or summon something to help them, they'd make the same mistakes Blade was.

So they were taking the longer, harder route. And Cheyenne would be with them every step of the way.

She might not have the physical strength to do it, but she had the mental fortitude.

And, for some reason, she was connected to whatever Blade was doing.

As she leaned into Max's side, content in the quietness between them, she just hoped she was enough.

CHEYENNE THRASHED IN HER SLEEP, the dream coming on hard. Blade stood over her, the stiletto in his hand shining in the waning moonlight. She tried to scream, but nothing came out. Blade's face looked half man, half wolf, as if he were mid-shift and hadn't realized it. It was such a grotesque image that she had to swallow down the bile in her throat. Though she didn't know if she was doing that in real life or only in her dream. She knew this was a nightmare, knew this was a figment of memory that might be real. Or perhaps it was the culmination of everything mixed together.

Blade glared at her before he spoke. "You were supposed to die. But now that you're alive, you will be used. You were the connection. You were the savior. You were the death."

She frowned, knowing he hadn't said that to her before, not when he loomed over her and tried to kill her. He had come so close to ending her, so close to snuffing out her life and her future. But the moon goddess had stepped in to save her. Cheyenne knew that now with such certainty that she wasn't even sure where it had come from.

Max and the others had been the ones to tell her that it was the moon goddess who had saved her. But she hadn't quite believed it. Yet with all the magic in the world, the one who saved her was the one who had started it all. At least in the lore of wolf shifters—everything began with the moon goddess.

The deity had seen a hunter kill a wolf for sport, and she became enraged. She forced the soul of that wolf into the body of the human, so both human and wolf had to share. The balance that came from that act had forced the man and wolf to figure out exactly who they were together. And that was the first wolf shifter.

The Talons came from that line. Cheyenne knew that there was more to the story, something about reincarnation and the fact that Parker was actually descended from that bloodline. But all that mattered to her right then was the fact that Blade was telling her something, and it wasn't what he had told her when everything actually happened.

She'd been given this dream for a reason, and even though she wasn't one to believe in prophecies and magic, she had seen them all with her own eyes.

And she couldn't ignore it anymore.

"I will kill everybody if I can. You were the sacrifice. You were the death. You were everything. And now, you're in my way. If you're still here, my plan cannot succeed. When you are gone, I will rule. The weak will perish. And everyone else will bow before me."

Cheyenne woke up screaming, her hands shaking. Max was sitting right beside her, his shirtless body so close to hers she could feel the heat of him. They had gone to sleep as soon as they got back to the house, exhausted from studying. But now, Cheyenne was wide-awake, her heart racing, and her palms clammy.

"It was a dream. It was a dream, but it wasn't a dream." She put her hands over her face, trying to control her breathing.

The room glowed gold from Max's eyes, and she knew that his wolf was at the forefront, but there wasn't anything she could do about that. She needed to calm herself so she could tell him exactly what had happened in her nightmare and both of them could calm down. Or, both of them could get angry and not calm down at all.

"What was the dream? Are you hurt?"

She looked over at him, lowering her hands. "I can be hurt from a dream?"

He shrugged and kissed her forehead. She loved the fact that he kept kissing her, touching her. She kept doing the same to him. She was still learning him, and he was learning her. They were drawn to each other. That was the bond between them. They had started this mating thing at the end instead of the beginning, but they were finding their way.

And she knew she wouldn't be able to deal with any of this without him. For such an independent woman, that scared her to death.

"I don't know if you can get hurt from a dream, but with everything that has gone on with my family? I don't doubt it. There's magic out there that can take a soul, that can break a bond, that could probably take over the world. The witches in our Pack are strong, some of the strongest out there. I trust those in the Coven now that I know them, and the members that tried to betray us were weeded out. But I didn't trust that witch who worked with Blade. And though she's dead, he probably has more of her ilk waiting in the wings. So, are you hurt?"

"No. But let me tell you what happened."

Cheyenne told him about the dream, told him the words that Blade had said, word for word. Max's eyes widened, and though he didn't take notes, she knew he was remembering every single little thing so they could tell Gideon and the others. There was truly no privacy anymore, not when it came to protecting the Pack. Her Pack.

"I don't like the sound of that. I don't like the sound of any of that."

"You think I like it? I don't like the fact that he kept using the words *sacrifice* and *death*. I don't like that I'm connected to it. Those men died, and I felt it. Gideon's power was taken from him, and it was like it was sent through me. And that scares me. Because if we have to destroy the artifact..."

She didn't finish the statement. She needed to let her thoughts come together. But Max didn't wait for her to continue. "Don't finish that. Don't even think it."

"But, what if I have to? What if I need to die for the artifact to be destroyed. What if, for us to survive, for the rest of the world to survive, the one thing that's connected to the artifact—other than Blade himself—has to be no more?"

Max growled, gripping her arm so tightly she thought she might bruise. Then, he let her go and kissed both shoulders. He hadn't gripped her on the left, hadn't been able to, but he still pressed his arm against her.

"Fuck, no. We're not going to let that happen. Do you understand me? I'm not going to let them take you. I just found you. Your friends love you. You're mine. Do you get that?"

"I don't think it's going to be a choice that either of us has. If it means saving the Pack and getting rid of the artifact? Then I'm going to do what I have to."

Max just stared at her before he lowered his lips to hers and kissed her.

Since neither of them was wearing many clothes, he quickly ripped his shirt from her body. She'd liked wearing it, liked being enveloped in his scent.

He plunged his fingers between her thighs, priming her so quickly she bucked off the bed, her fingers digging into his shoulders and upper arms so hard, she knew if he weren't a shifter, she would have probably left bruises.

He pumped his fingers in and out of her in rapid succession and, before she knew it, she was coming on his hand and trying not to scream so loudly the neighbors heard her call out his name.

"You're mine," he growled, nipping her on the shoulder where he'd bitten her before. It was still tender, but whenever he touched it, she almost came.

Damn wolf.

Damn man.

He sat up suddenly, lifting her and putting her on her knees so she faced the wall with her hands clinging to the headrest.

"Hold on."

"Max." It was a gasp. Needy.

"You're mine," he repeated, slamming into her. Her body shook, and she was ready to come from the intrusion alone. "Just like I'm yours." Another slam. "Take me. I'm yours. Take me. You're mine. But you can't stop. Can't let go. We're ours."

Then he was pounding in and out of her, his right arm holding her close while his left hand played with her nipples.

She came again, this time so hard she had to close her eyes. Her pussy was so tender, so charged that she came *again* just because he moved her while she was still coming.

And when he filled her once more, he bit her again, marking her as his. She reached around, digging her fingers into his skin, wanting to mark him as hers, as well.

She was so damn scared of what was to come, but right then, all she had was Max.

Right then, all she had was who they could be together.

And maybe, just maybe, with this feeling—with this need—they could face whatever came.

No matter the cost.

CHAPTER ELEVEN

Cheyenne looked down at her hands, wondering if she would ever feel normal again. Of course, she didn't know exactly what *normal* was anymore. The night before, she'd had an odd prophecy-drenched nightmare and ended up having angry and emotional sex with Max as she tried to forget what the word *sacrifice* meant.

"You look like you're lost," Dawn said, leaning into her.

The four of them—Dawn, Cheyenne, Aimee, and Dhani—were taking a break from their various training and duties, and Cheyenne's research so they could talk and try to find some of that normal again.

"I'm okay. Okay, not okay. And I just said okay a lot." She pinched the bridge of her nose and leaned into her friend. "I guess I'm not."

"You had a lot happen to you in a short amount of

time. I wouldn't be surprised if you were in the middle of a nervous breakdown." Dhani winced as the rest of her friends looked at her. "That sounded better in my head than it did aloud."

Aimee sighed and wrapped her arm around Dhani's neck, jokingly choking her before letting go. The fact that it was Aimee who did it and not the others just showed Cheyenne how much her friend had healed and grown in the months since mating Walker.

"Considering what each of us has gone through in the past couple of years, I'm surprised we're not all in the middle of a nervous breakdown. However, Cheyenne? We're all here for you. We might not be in your exact situation, but each of us has gone through something. So we're here to listen."

Dawn sighed. "I mean, I had to deal with finding a new Pack, making my old Pack an actual legitimate one, finding a mate who didn't really want to want me because he already had one—or at least had the potential to have one. And then I dealt with the fact that our world really wasn't at the end of the war." Dawn looked over at her and frowned, "Well, I guess if you put all that together, it's kind of scary. But we made it through. And my mate loves me. And, eventually, when this war is over, we're going to have a baby."

Cheyenne's eyes widened, and she looked at her friend. "You're pregnant?"

Dawn shook her head, holding up her hands to try and

stem the excitement. "No, I'm not pregnant. But Mitchell and I decided it was time to start trying. Okay, maybe not time to start trying right now since we're attempting to kill an evil overlord."

The four of them laughed, though it was tension-filled. They were trying to find some happiness in the darkness, but it wasn't always easy when Blade had literally tried to kill each and every one of them—and had nearly succeeded all four times.

Dawn continued. "But we're ready to make that decision. And I think when Blade is gone, we're going to start a family. Even if another Pack comes at us, even if another demon comes, even if the world threatens to end all over again. We're going to try. Because we need something to fight for. And the future is it."

Cheyenne wrapped her arms around her friend and couldn't help but smile.

"You're going to be an amazing mother. You're also a maternal dominant, and that means you're already wonderful with children. You have this innate sense of motherhood and goodness and caring. And you're going to fight no matter what happens. You're going to be the most protective mom you can be. And I guess we're sisters-in-law. I think that just hit me."

Dawn grinned. "I know. I know that all the others are actual siblings, but Mitchell and Max are the only two brothers in their branch of the family. So I guess we're finally sisters. Although I kind of thought the three of you were already my sisters."

Aimee laughed. "Well, I guess that means that Dhani is my sister-in-law. But then so is Brie, Leah, and Avery. And Parker and Brandon are my brothers-in-law. Those tend to add up when there are six siblings, and one of them is in a triad."

"Just wait until everybody starts having children," Dhani said with a laugh. "I mean, Max and Mitchell's parents might've stopped at two, but it seems most people in this den like to have like twelve kids."

Cheyenne snorted and shook her head. "Maybe not twelve, but a lot of them have like eight. Even over in the Redwoods that seems to be the normal amount." She crossed her legs and winced at that thought. "I don't think I really want to imagine having eight children. Maybe not even one. Do wolves have pets? Could we start with a nice pet? Because I am a vet, after all, and sometimes I just want a puppy. Or a kitten. Or a turtle. Turtles live long. That could work, right?" Then Cheyenne froze, and bile filled her throat as the ramifications of the situation set in. "No, I guess having a pet wouldn't work out. Because shifters live for so long, and having to watch their pets die after, what, ten years? No, I guess pets don't work out."

Dawn reached out and gripped her hand. "It's the case sometimes. But, other times, they have pets. There aren't that many in this den, but the Redwoods have a few. I think it just depends on where the person is in their life. A lot of the Talons are over a century old, and having pets really isn't what they need. Then again, maybe a pet is exactly what an elder needs. That way, they can remember their mortality. Because without that, without that desire to live so brightly within those short years, sometimes it makes it hard to imagine what life is worth."

Aimee leaned forward and brushed Cheyenne's hair from her face. "Are we going to talk about the elephant in the room?"

That made Cheyenne laugh, and she had to explain to them the elephant versus wolf joke that she had with Max.

"I don't know when I'm going to change. I know it has to happen because I'm not a witch, and shifting just doesn't happen magically. I can't just stay with Max and not hurt him if I'll eventually fade away. But I don't think I'm ready for that shift. I know it's going to hurt, and frankly, I want Blade to be dead first."

Dhani shook her head. "It will hurt. At least that's what they tell me. I got lucky that I'm a witch."

"By lucky you mean you almost died because your powers were bound?" Cheyenne asked.

"Okay, so I wasn't lucky."

Aimee shrugged. "I lived because of being changed. But my change was much different than anyone else's." Aimee was a lion shifter because of Audrey. Walker hadn't been strong enough to change her because Aimee had been so far gone that they needed the most dominant wolf around to complete the change. Audrey was damn dominant, but she was a lion. Cheyenne didn't know if Max had been dominant enough to save her, but the moon goddess had stepped in anyway.

"I don't know if the Pack is really going to give you an option," Dawn put in, and Cheyenne narrowed her eyes.

"What do you mean by that?" Cheyenne asked.

"All I mean is that you're a liability in some's eyes. And a few of the elders won't like that. With Gideon as our Alpha, we have to go with some of the old traditions. Although that was how it was in the Pack before I was even born—the Centrals that is. So, for all I know, they're not going to let that happen. But to keep you safe, maybe being a wolf would be the best for you. Because I'm not saying you're weak, but you're not strong enough to protect yourself right now. And I never want to take that choice from you, but if the war goes on for too long, and if it gets any more dangerous than it already is? You might have to rethink that timetable of yours."

"I don't want to talk about this right now," Cheyenne put in. "Let's go for our walk before we go get something to eat. Okay?" She stood up quickly from the bench, and her friends joined her. "I'm not running from the situation, I'm putting it on hold so I can worry about the end of the world and Blade rather than my own sense of humanity. Okay?"

Dawn leaned over and hugged her close. "I still have a sense of humanity. Even if I wasn't born human. But when you're ready, we'll be here to talk. And we'll make sure you're as prepared as possible. Because you're my sister. One of my best friends. And I'm so happy, in a sick way, that I'm not going to have to watch you fade away. Because we know that you were walking away from us to save us and yourself. But mostly because you care about us. So, I just want to make sure you know that we love you."

Cheyenne moved away so she could wipe the tears from her face before opening her arms. All three of her friends moved close and hugged her tight. These ladies were some of the strongest women she knew. They had been through their ups and downs, had been through their own pains and losses, but they were her family.

She didn't have a family in the outside world. She had no one. Her practice was already in another person's hands, and soon, she would sign over the paperwork so it was no longer hers at all. She hadn't even had a chance to truly say goodbye. But it wasn't safe for her and, frankly, it wasn't safe for anyone else for her to be out there. Kameron's and Mitchell's wolves had left the den to go and pick up her stuff.

They had packed up everything from her apartment and moved it into Max's house. Her house. It'd been two weeks since everything had changed. And it seemed like it had only been a blink. A breath.

But she couldn't look back, not if she wanted to remain sane.

So she and her friends started walking back towards to

the center of the den where most of the people were. Cheyenne knew that there were people on patrol all around them at all times. And a lot of them had likely heard their conversation since shifter hearing was far more enhanced than that of humans. She really wanted to get into the whys of that and even the math and science behind it.

And later when she wasn't studying to figure out what the artifact was and what it could do and how to stop it, she would be able to talk with Walker and Leah about it. Because she needed a place within this Pack. She was a vet, and she loved animals.

The fact that she was mated to a wolf had its own sense of irony. But it wasn't as if wolves really needed a vet within their ranks. Maybe she could be a doctor if Walker needed more help. Or she'd find another way. Because she needed to fit in, and she needed to not just be Max's mate.

Not that there was anything *just* about that. It was all so new, and Cheyenne wasn't used to what everything felt like. It was weird because if she closed her eyes and focused, she could almost sense exactly where Max was in the den. She knew he was training with some of the other sentries, making sure everybody was keeping their skills honed for the battle to come.

Because there would be a battle. There had to be.

There had been small skirmishes up until now when it came to Blade. But everything always ended in bloodshed.

There would be no diplomacy, no letters of promise and intent when it came to finishing this.

That wasn't how shifters worked, and even in the final battle with the humans, there was a tank. There was bloodshed.

She held back her anger. Max had still been hurt because of it all.

"You're thinking too hard over there again," Aimee said from her other side.

Cheyenne shook herself from her thoughts and tried to pay attention to exactly what her friends were saying. They were all discussing what needed to happen within the den since it was becoming harder and harder for them to leave and actually live within the human world. Apparently, over time, they had built their own infrastructure within the den wards. It made it so humans couldn't easily come in and out of the territory, but it also made it so wolves sometimes felt like they were trapped. And a trapped wolf was never a good idea.

But they were making things work out. They had their own farms, grain houses, even their own cattle. Though how a shifter could deal with cows, Cheyenne didn't really understand. She figured it likely had to do with the witches in the group. There were schools, stores, and homes for everyone. Although there were a lot more barracks than there used to be, the single wolves having been pulled back into the den during the human war, and now being forced back because of the Aspens.

Every time peace seemed to be unfolding, something else came in to disrupt it. Cheyenne hoped that there could be breathing room for everyone soon, but just taking these stolen moments with her friends was pretty much the only thing they could do at this time.

They were just turning the corner when the sound of a startled yelp reached her ears. Cheyenne was off running even before her supernatural friends were. She ran through the trees, almost tripped over a rock, and leapt over a fallen log, her friends passing her along the way. She didn't care if she was the slow human. It had sounded like a pup. A little kid was hurt, and if her friends were running as well, she was going to help.

"Cheyenne, we need you. Aimee, go get help. Go get one of the sentries." Dawn shouted out orders as Cheyenne scrambled her way to where Dawn and Dhani surrounded a child in wolf form, bleeding from the back of his thigh, his little mouth making mewling sounds.

Tears sprang to her eyes, but she pushed them back, knowing she had to help and try not to act as if she were scared. She was a vet, she helped animals all the time. Just because this baby wolf pup also happened to be a human child half the time, didn't mean that she would change the way she treated him.

"Let me see what we're dealing with," she said, her voice brisk. It had to be.

She went to her knees, the damp soil clinging to her. They'd had rain the night before, and now everything was wet. She had a feeling this little pup had strayed from school, and while people were probably looking for him, it looked as if he had rolled a bit down the wet incline.

The little boy looked at her fingers, and she ran her hand through his fur. "I know you can understand me, baby. Do you want to stay in this form, or would it help to shift?" She looked up at Dawn as she asked that, hoping it was the right question.

"How about you stay in your wolf form, baby. Cheyenne will be able to help you here. And as soon as Aimee gets Walker, he's going to be able to Heal you, okay? It doesn't look that bad at all. You're super strong and very brave. Okay, baby? Are you listening to me, Mark?"

"Okay, Mark, I'm just going to take a look at your leg. I'm sure you're fine, okay, baby?"

Mark licked Cheyenne's fingers, and she smiled at him. She had worked with a wolf before, and plenty of puppies. But working with one who could actually understand you? This was a whole new ballgame.

She felt around and looked at the wound. She was pretty sure Mark had broken his leg and also had a few abrasions. He hadn't lost a lot of blood and would be fine. She wasn't sure what Walker could do as Healer versus her as just a human vet.

"Walker can't Heal a bone, he has to set it first," Dhani whispered in her ear so the injured little pup couldn't hear.

"I'm going to set it then, and then he can Heal away all

the pain." She whispered the words back, but she knew Dhani had heard, as well as Dawn.

Dawn began singing a soft song, the baby almost falling to sleep. Dawn was a maternal dominant wolf, and Cheyenne knew that the woman was not only calming this little pup but also using her powers and bonds that connected her with the Pack to hopefully take away some of his pain. Her friend wasn't a Healer, but she was meant for her place in this Pack.

Dhani quickly looked around for two branches after Cheyenne asked for them, knowing they wouldn't have to use them for long, but she still wanted to make sure everything was set. She probably wouldn't use them at all since Walker was on his way, but she needed to be sure. And then she went about setting the bone, wincing at the sound it made, and even more so at the fact that the little baby let out another painful noise.

And then Walker was there, his hands on the wolf pup. He gave her a look of gratitude, and then there were two parents and two teachers running through the woods to come and see their little pup.

Apparently, a group of kids had been playing hide and seek, and Mark had hidden a little too well and fell down into the ravine. He'd tried to get back up but lost his way. People had been looking for him and had even been on their way to ask Cheyenne and the other girls for help.

But Cheyenne and the others had found him first.

"Thank you for starting the job, Cheyenne. You did

what I would've done at first. And the fact that Dawn was here to help take away his pain because she's been learning that trick as a maternal dominant helped everything. You did everything I would've done. And, frankly, when we finish with Blade, I'd love for you to come work with us. I know you haven't figured out exactly what you want to do within this Pack, but Leah and I could use you. You're a wonderful healer, and I know that you're a vet, and there will always be jokes, but you're family now. You're Pack. Welcome."

Warming from those words, Cheyenne found herself standing in the middle of a den, people walking all around her. But her eyes were only for Max. She felt like she was finally connected to something. Not only to the man walking towards her, but to the others who gave her nods of appreciation and came up to hug her and tell her thank you for helping with Mark. Word apparently spread fast when it came to the pups.

Max cupped her face in his hand and brushed his lips along hers. "I hear you've had a busy afternoon. Are you okay?"

She kissed his jaw and then leaned against his chest. "I was scared, but he's going to be okay. I just don't like the sounds when I have to set a bone."

"The moon goddess gave the maternals the ability to help with that pain," Max began. "Dawn is still new to using it, but she's getting better at it. And I bet at some point, Dhani will figure out if she can use her powers as a spirit witch to help. Knowing her, she's going to find a way to help all the children in this den. You did wonderful. Aimee found everybody in time. And you set the leg so Walker didn't have to break it before he Healed it. That's the problem with shifters, even pups who are just learning how to shift. We heal far too quickly, but not in the right way all the time." Max looked down at his arm, and she was aware that everyone around them was most likely able to hear, but he spoke anyway.

"Being a shifter and being able to heal saved my life. It couldn't save my arm, but I'm still here." He blew out a breath and changed the subject. "You did a good job. And Walker told me on the way here that he offered you a job. I'm kind of glad that he did because I was going to have to beat him up if he didn't."

She rolled her eyes. "You don't have to do that. I can stand up for myself."

"I know you can. But I guess that's what a mate is for. I don't really know, I'm still learning my way around this."

She smiled, but before she could say anything else, she threw back her head and screamed. Power surged through her, pouring out of her fingertips and her mouth. It felt like someone was taking a cattle prod and stabbing her over and over again. Electricity hummed through her body, and her blood felt as if it boiled. Max had his arms around her, and others were coming near to help or attack if needed. Cheyenne knew what was happening, though.

The artifact was in use.

And Blade had just killed someone else.

Power thrummed through her body, making her shake. She knew blood was seeping from her nose, her eyes, and even her mouth.

The artifact was killing her.

The power was too much for her human body to bear.

But there was no way she could stop it.

And then the power went away as quickly as it had come.

And she lay in Max's embrace, knowing she was helpless. Knowing that Blade had killed someone else. And knowing there was nothing she could do except try to find a way to use the connection against him or stop it altogether.

There had to be a way.

BLADE

Blade wiped the blood from his mouth and then turned away so he could make his way to his quarters before the others saw him. He'd killed two wolves from a Pack in the Midwest, stripping their Alpha's power for a few minutes before giving it back as a form of goodwill.

He shouldn't feel this weak. The only reason he'd killed any of the wolves at all was because he needed their lifeforce to hold onto the artifact. The damn stone was killing him. Taking off a year at a time, killing him breath by breath if he didn't find a way around it.

So, he killed the weak and stole their energy. That was how he was able to move at all right then. He would be fine soon, he always was, but there was something wrong.

Something was blocking him. Blocking the power.

He was supposed to be the Conduit, the strength.

And the only person who could be in his way was the one who should have died.

"That bitch," he growled, wiping the rest of the blood from his face.

Cinnamon...Cheyenne...his sacrifice had to be alive.

And was in his way.

"Not for long."

Not. For. Long.

CHAPTER TWELVE

"Want a beer?" Mitchell asked, his head in the fridge.

Max nodded and then realized he must be tired since Mitchell couldn't see him. Instead, he said, "Yeah."

His brother pulled out two, opened them, and handed one over to him before taking a drink of his. "Want to talk about it?"

"About what? The fact that my mate almost died in my arms? Again. Or the fact that Cheyenne and I are moving along at breakneck speed like nothing is wrong?"

Mitchell raised a brow. "First, that's how mating works. Or at least how it used to work. You find your potential mate, you follow the mating urge, you create the bond and, boom, you have to deal with all of the emotional and mental issues that come with falling for a person because of a paranormal bond before you fall for them like a human. We're not entirely human, Max. We're wolves. We go about things differently. Honestly, the fact that Cheyenne is going along with all of this like she is tells me that she's far stronger than I thought she was."

Max growled. "You thought my mate was weak?"

Mitchell rolled his eyes before taking a seat next to him on the couch. "You know that's not what I meant. You're just at the start of your mating, and you're territorial."

Max still growled just a little bit but tilted his beer towards his brother. "I'm having one of those days, maybe don't test me?"

"Considering you're letting me test you at all, I think that counts as progress."

Max didn't say anything to that, and really wasn't in the mood or ready to deal with any of it. He knew his brother wasn't pushing at him on purpose, he was doing it out of care. Trying to see if Max was healed and ready to be part of the family again. But Max needed some time to figure out exactly who he was, and who he was with Cheyenne before he stopped hiding in the shadows.

"Are the others coming? Or are we heading to the elders' house to meet them there?" Max was at Mitchell's place, having some brother time before they went to the elders' area and met with Xavier and the rest. It seemed the elders needed to talk with the Brentwoods—and Cheyenne especially.

Max didn't know why that sent chills down his spine, but maybe it had to do with the fact that the elders were searching—along with Cheyenne and Max—for information about the origins of the artifact and what it meant for the present. And considering that his mate was tightly connected to that? He wasn't sure he wanted any of the answers.

"The cousins are coming here, at least the men are. We're going to meet the women there. Brie and the others wanted some girl time before they had to say goodbye to the kids and meet us for the family meeting. Although, is it really a family meeting when we have to meet with the elders?"

"Yeah, I guess it's not really just family when we have to deal with the end of the world."

"You're saying meeting with the elders is the end of the world?"

"It sure feels like it some days." Max let out a breath, using his thumb to peel back the label on the beer bottle. He needed something to do, and he was too stressed to think about what was really important. Even as he thought that, the only things on his mind were Cheyenne and the fact that she had almost died the day before. "She almost died, Mitchell." His voice cracked, and he didn't bother clearing his throat.

His brother was silent for a moment before he finally spoke. "I know. And I know it must have hurt you to be there, to hold her during that. But she's okay right now. And we're going to find a way to fix this."

"I don't know about that. I want to believe in happily ever afters and fate and all of that, but it's hard to when I saw what happened to every single one of you when you found your mates. The world keeps coming at us, keeps trying to pull us apart. We've lost friends, family, we've lost so many in the wars. It's hard to believe that there can be peace when every time we turn around, a new enemy tries to take it away. I thought we were finally safe after our dad died, after our uncles finally died. And then we heard about that demon attacking the Redwood Pack. We didn't lose anyone in that battle, but the Redwoods lost so much."

Mitchell nodded. "And they're stronger now, although the scars run deep."

"So deep that you can see it in their eyes sometimes. I mean, Brynn almost lost her mate even before she met him because of it. And then she almost lost him again because of it later." Brynn was their cousin, who had mated into the Redwood Pack.

We all have scars, some more than others." Mitchell gave him a pointed look, but Max just shrugged. He knew his scars, knew they weren't going away even with magic. There were some things that wolves just couldn't heal.

"And then we had years of peace after the Redwoods found theirs. And then the humans came, all because of our uncle, Leo."

"He was the one who started it, but I think, in the end, humans would've found out who we were no matter what. It's too hard to hide, and too many of the wrong people knew the magic existed. I think...give us a couple more decades, it'll be good. I want my children to be able to live in a world where they don't have to hide who they are. And I know that seems far-fetched, but maybe it can actually happen one day."

"I want your children to have that, as well."

"Do you not want kids, then?"

"I never thought I would have them. I don't know. I always felt like I was going to be the fun uncle. Even before everything changed and I lost my hand. I just never saw a mate in my future. I was already happy. Now, it just feels like it was so long ago that that person was me. I don't know what Cheyenne wants. I don't think we're there yet. We're still trying to figure out how our human halves work together even though my wolf is already ready for her. But she's dying, Mitchell. Every time it hits her, it takes her longer to recover, and it's slowly draining her life from her. She's dying because I can't figure out how to disconnect her from that artifact. And I know that she wants to find a way to use that power against Blade, but I don't know if she's strong enough. Hell, I don't know if *I'm* strong enough."

And that scared him more than he wanted to admit. He had spent so long trying to figure out how to put himself back together, he wasn't sure he'd done it right.

He wasn't sure that he could find the strength to do what had to be done to keep his Pack safe.

Because if he had to lose his mate after just finding her to stop the end of the world? He wasn't sure he would be on the right side of history.

But that wasn't something he could tell Mitchell, not that he didn't believe his brother hadn't already figured out what he was thinking anyway. Mitchell would die for Dawn, would sacrifice anything.

But would any of his family members sacrifice the Pack to save their mates?

That, he didn't know. And Max didn't know the answer for himself either.

Before they could get any deeper into their conversation, the rest of the Brentwood men showed up as one, as if they'd all left at the same time. Gideon looked ready to punch something, but his cousin, his Alpha, didn't appreciate being summoned. Even if it was Xavier and the other elders, Gideon did not like to be told what to do unless it had to do with Brie. He figured that Brie was the only one who dared to tell Gideon what to do on a daily basis, even though their wolves were so different.

Finn was there, as well, surprising Max. Finn was the Redwood Heir but was over with the Talon Pack often. His cousin-in-law scented of Brynn and the baby, Mackenzie. Max figured that they had left their daughter at home with the other Redwoods. Goddess knew there were enough children over there—enough for an army.

Since Brynn wasn't with Finn, Max knew that his cousin was likely with the other women for their alone time. Ryder came in behind Finn, a frown on his face, but he didn't look as angry as Gideon. Ryder was usually off in his own little world, and when his cousin looked over his shoulder, Max figured it had to do with what Ryder saw in the shadows. Ryder could see death, which always worried Max, but if anyone could handle it, it was Ryder.

Two other members joined them in the room that weren't Brentwoods. Shane and Bram were lieutenants, who not only worked for Kameron under his role as the Enforcer but were part of Gideon's guard, as well. They had pretty much become family over time, and since their mate was Charlotte, who was Finn's cousin, they were one big, happy family.

Max was pretty sure he needed a family tree in order to figure out who was related to whom, but in the end, they were all Talons or connected to them.

Parker and Brandon walked in hand in hand in the middle of the conversation, although Max heard the word *"Avery"* muttered under Parker's breath, so they had to be talking about their mate. It wasn't uncommon for triads to happen in werewolf Packs, and the fact that they'd had two in such a short timeframe just told Max that their Pack was growing stronger.

Walker and Kameron came in at the end, also conversing—about a sports team of all things. How anyone had time to talk about sports in a world where their lives seemed on the precipice all the time, Max didn't know. But he also knew that Walker and Kameron were constantly on call, and always leaving their warm beds and their mates every night. So, if they needed to talk about something silly that had nothing to do with the dangers surrounding them, Max would let them be.

There was so much testosterone in the room, Max knew Cheyenne would have probably made a joke about it if she were here. He missed her, and he'd seen her less than an hour ago. He didn't like to be away from her, not when everything was so fresh and raw. He'd almost lost her, and it had taken Walker actually Healing her to make her okay again. Max's hand had been covered in blood, his mate's blood, and Cheyenne had just looked at him, her eyes wide with pain.

One of the Packs in the Midwest had contacted them to let them know that they'd lost another set of wolves, all thanks to Blade. Their Alpha had lost his power before he'd been given it back. It seemed that Blade was going through each Pack, one by one, showing his might.

And some of the weaker Packs were already thinking of buckling. Honestly, Max didn't blame them, not when they didn't have the strength and numbers to fight back.

Things seemed pretty bleak, and if he and Cheyenne and the elders weren't quick about it, they may start losing some Packs to Blade and his so-called Supreme Alpha title.

"Does anyone know what this meeting is about?"

Kameron asked, a beer in his hand. In fact, every single one of them had a beer in hand, even though not all of them were truly drinking it. They just needed something to do, something to have in their hands. Although there were no more sports conversations, just discussions about elder meetings and the end of the world. Because that was their life now. In fact, that was how their life had been for far too long.

"I don't know, but I think it has to do with our newest member," Gideon put in, turning towards Max. Max kept Gideon's gaze for a moment before lowering his eyes. He might be strong, might be dominant, but he was nowhere near Gideon's power.

"I don't like the fact that it feels like it's a show, but that's the elders for you," Max muttered. "I just want to know what they found because Cheyenne and I haven't found a single thing."

"We're going to figure this out," Brandon said, his voice soft. Max's cousin was the Omega. And Max knew that Brandon was slowly leaching the fear and the tension from the room, pulling it into himself through the bonds. Parker had his arm around Brandon, steadying his mate. Max couldn't feel Brandon work on him, probably because he was so tense, his defenses in place so much that Brandon couldn't reach him. Brandon looked at him, and Max shook his head. He didn't want help, not then. He let his cousin in occasionally on the battlefield, but it wasn't often. Max needed time. Time to heal. Time to think. And he needed the emotions. He couldn't focus if he didn't have those feelings pushing at him.

"We're going to take Blade out, no matter what." Gideon's pronouncement wasn't anything new, but for some reason, it worried Max. Because he knew that every single person in the room had a feeling Cheyenne was fully connected to the artifact.

And if they had to get rid of the artifact, what if that meant they had to get rid of her?

They met up with their mates on the way to the elder meeting. The elders were located on the opposite end of the den from Max's home. They had their own little space away from children and the other Pack members who might harm them. It wasn't that they were in any physical danger, more mental. The elders had so much history in their minds, so much power in their veins. It had nothing to do with dominance, just age itself, and sometimes being around others was too much for them. Things had changed over time, Xavier for one. But it was still hard for the elders to be around so many wolves at once.

And considering there were so many Brentwoods right then, Max wasn't sure how long this meeting would last.

Cheyenne sat next to him on one of the logs around the firepit. They wouldn't be going into the homes today. Instead, they were meeting outside in a group as if they were camping instead of talking about the end of days and artifacts.

Max had his hand on Cheyenne's, their fingers

entwined. Normally, he'd never let his fighting hand be taken like this, but with his family surrounding him, he felt safe.

Safe from outside forces, but not from the knowledge that filled Xavier's eyes and what might be revealed while they warmed near a fire.

Cheyenne was in trouble.

He knew that deep down in his bones.

And his mate did, as well.

"What is it, Xavier?" Gideon asked. "Why are we here?"

Xavier didn't look at the Alpha as he spoke, neither did the four other elders who sat quietly as they let Xavier be the spokesperson for their group. Xavier looked directly at Cheyenne and Max.

"The artifact is killing Cheyenne."

The others didn't speak, and since Max's wolf was in his throat, he wasn't sure he could either. But Cheyenne found her voice.

"I figured." She didn't sound nonchalant about it, but as if she'd accepted her fate, or at least considered succumbing to it.

Max would damn well fight her on that idea.

"You seem to be a Conduit," Xavier put in.

Max nodded, squeezing Cheyenne's hand. "Because every time Blade uses the power, she feels it."

"Like it's going through me, pulling at everything I

have. Some goes back to him, but then it flies back into me." Cheyenne swallowed hard and leaned into him.

The fact that she did so in front of everyone made Max want to howl. She didn't like looking weak, but then again, needing to lean on others wasn't weak at all.

"And each time he does, you fall harder, faster. Your humanity isn't enough to keep you alive if Blade uses the artifact again."

"So, I need to become wolf." Max squeezed her hand again as she spoke. What he really wanted to do was pick her up and run away. Hide her from this choice that wasn't a choice at all. "I knew I would have to eventually. That's how it works when you mate into a Pack."

"But there's no true choice. Not anymore." Max knew he'd growled the words, but he couldn't help it, not when his mate was in danger.

"There isn't. She needs to be wolf. Now."

"Okay. Just tell me when." Max heard the worry in her voice, but he wasn't sure anyone else could, not even her best friends, who looked at her with their emotions clear in their eyes. They loved her, they were her family, and Max knew they were scared, as well.

"Tomorrow, then," Gideon said quietly, his voice a dominant growl. "Tonight...you can have tonight." He looked at Max for a moment before turning to Cheyenne.

Fear filled Max, but he tried to breathe through it so Cheyenne wouldn't be able to tell.

Because to become a wolf meant killing a part of your humanity.

To become a wolf, you had to almost die.

And not all those who tried actually survived.

No matter their strength.

His mate could die tomorrow.

But tonight... they at least had tonight.

CHAPTER THIRTEEN

Cheyenne kissed her mate, knowing he was scared for her, but she couldn't feel her fear. Not then. She was numb. Too numb.

"I need to feel," she whispered against his lips.

"Then let me help you."

So he kissed her again and backed her up to the bed. They were alone, having left the others along the way. There would be time for more talking and fears later.

Right now, it was about her mate, her Max.

The man she never saw coming.

The man she was falling for.

Slowly, they stripped each other, their bodies moving as one as they learned each other once again. It wasn't like the first time, or even any of the times after. This was just for them, just what they needed.

He kissed her lips, her neck, her breasts, and kept

kissing her, kept loving her. This could be their last time, they both knew it, but they weren't focusing on that. They couldn't.

Instead, she went to her knees in front of him, pushing his hand away when he went to pull her back. She wanted to do this for him, wanted to feel him in her mouth.

She licked the tip of his cock, sucking and flicking her tongue. Max groaned, tangling his fingers in her hair as he rocked his hips ever so slightly. She opened her mouth wider and took him deeper, wanting him, all of him.

But he was too big for her to take fully, so she used her hands to work the rest, bobbing her head and flattening her tongue as she hummed down his shaft. He growled, pumping his hips a little harder, and she took it, needing all of him. As much as she could take.

And when he came, he pulled back slightly so she didn't choke, but she still swallowed all of him up, wanting more.

Then she was on her back, and Max was between her legs, licking at and eating her cunt, fucking her with his fingers hard enough that she came on his face in no time at all. Max loved eating pussy and whispered it often in the mornings before he moved between her legs to wake her up.

And the man was damn good at it.

Then he was over her, his cock poised to enter her, already hard again thanks to shifter genetics.

She shook her head, though. "My turn to be on top."

He gave her a wicked grin that went straight to her heart before he flipped them both over. She found herself on top of him, her wet heat sliding along his rigid length. Then she sheathed herself, his thickness stretching her in the best way possible. As soon as she was seated, she put her hands on his chest, her fingers digging into his skin but not in any way that would remind him of the terrible things in his past, and she *moved*.

She braced herself over him, her hair creating a curtain for them both as she rocked against him. He lifted his hips slightly, pumping in and out of her, and they made love, slowly and just for them.

And when they came, she collapsed on top of him, needing him—just the feel of him, all of him.

She knew change was once again coming, but with Max, she was ready.

Finally.

CHEYENNE FOUND herself standing in Walker's clinic but not in a room she'd ever been in before. There were chains on the wall, and thick leather belts on a metal bed that looked like some torture device rather than something meant for comfort.

She knew that she was going to have to be bitten, a lot. She also knew that it would hurt. Gideon was going to do it himself, the strongest wolf of the Pack, perhaps in the entire area—except for Blade.

Although nobody really knew Blade's dominance anymore, not when he'd used dark magic and had hidden from others. It was Blade's Pack that made him strong, much like Gideon said it was the Talons that made him dominant.

But Gideon was dominant all by himself.

He was pure dominance.

And that meant he had the greatest chance of making sure Cheyenne didn't die from the transformation.

She wouldn't be able to have any pain meds, wouldn't be able to be held or comforted. Because she didn't want to end up hurting anyone. She didn't want to move the wrong way and bleed out. It was a barbaric way to be transitioned into a new world, but then again, she *was* losing her humanity. At least a part of it.

Maybe there needed to be bloodshed for something that was so much the opposite of who she was currently, of who the other people in this room were.

Maybe she needed all of that so there could be a firm line between before and after.

Because she didn't have a firm grasp of what had been before she knew about shifters. Of what was before she knew that Dawn was a wolf and Cheyenne was introduced to the Packs. It had all blurred, much like everything before Max—and after. Because Cheyenne had known him before she was mated to him, by first the moon goddess, and then by their choice.

She had known him and fought beside him. Now, she

had to realize exactly what it meant to be a part of this Pack and not the outsider.

"Are you going to be okay?" Max put his arm around her waist. Because he did, she felt him physically wince after his words. "No, you're not going to be okay. And I shouldn't have asked that question. We can wait a couple of days if you want, we can find a way to make this work."

She leaned against him, needing his touch. She hadn't needed touch before him, but with Max? She couldn't help but crave it. There was no looking back when it came to Max. Or her future.

"No, today's the day. We always knew this day would come. We always knew that I would have to become a wolf."

"Because you're my mate. In order to stay my mate, you need to become a shifter. Because I don't want to watch you die. I *can't* watch you die."

Cheyenne turned in his arms and rested her head on his chest. She didn't understand how she could feel so close to him so quickly. But she couldn't let go of him. She couldn't do anything without thinking of him. He was in her heart, the bond so strong, she could feel him everywhere she went. She might not be able to feel his emotions or always know exactly where he was in the den. She couldn't speak to him across the bond like some wolves could. She didn't have any other special powers. But she could feel his presence within her, even if he was far away. Even if the moon goddess had made the choice for them at first, there was no going back. And so she told him that.

"There's no going back. And I don't want to go back. We can only move forward, and I'm going to do that with you. If that means I have to be a wolf and go through everything that doing that entails along the way, I will. Aimee got through it, even in the worst situation, and she wasn't prepared at all. Dawn might have been born a wolf, but she had to go through a first shift. And Dhani had to go through her own transformation when her powers were unlocked, when she sacrificed herself to save us all. They might not be in this room right now because I didn't want them to have to watch this, but they're in my heart. And now, Max, are you sure you can be in here?"

They were the only two in the room for now. Walker, Leah, Gideon, and a couple of the other brothers would be in soon. Cheyenne didn't want everyone to see her at her weakest, and she didn't want them to see Max at his. But her mate had insisted on being in the room, and that meant that others would likely have to hold him back.

Because she knew him, knew how he would react. He would want to come after Gideon for what was about to happen. And they could not stop the transformation mid-progression.

She had heard stories from some of the other mates in the Redwood and Talon Packs about how mates who watched the process in a controlled setting needed to be held back, no matter their dominance. Even the most submissive wolves would fight. Their wolves did not want to watch their mates in distress, even if the outcome was for the best.

That was just how their world worked, and that meant they had to work harder to make sure Cheyenne survived this.

"I'm not leaving you. So you're going to be stuck with me." He kissed her nose, and she smiled. He made her smile, even now.

"I think the whole point is that you'll be stuck with me."

Because the elders were right. She had felt herself fading the last time the artifact was used. And she knew Blade was just raring to use it again. And while he might be a very dominant wolf, she was just a human. Not that there was anything simple about being a human. It was more that she couldn't survive what might come next without having extra strength. And if having a new part of herself allowed her to live to help take down Blade and help the Talon Pack, then she would deal with whatever pain came.

"I know it's going to hurt, but I'm going to be here with you. No matter what." Max kissed her again, and then the others walked into the room.

Walker strode up to her and put his hand on her shoulder. She pulled away from Max so she could hug him. He was a Healer, and she knew he didn't like to see anybody in pain without being able to help. "You have to stop getting that look on your face, Walker. I know there's nothing you can do. We've talked about this."

"You say that, but I'm going to repeat myself anyway. I can't use my Healing abilities, not during the physical attack. After Gideon is finished..." He cleared his throat since the idea of ripping into flesh wasn't the easiest thing to talk about. "I can help with the ruins. But I have to be careful so I don't Heal you so much that the shifting doesn't actually happen. We need that change to snap into place. With you so connected to Max already, we should be able to tell if it worked right away. So we'll be able to help you survive to get to that point, but you have to be the one to get us to the point where I can help you. Okay? You have to be strong. You have to be strong for yourself. For Max. And for the girls I know are probably standing right outside this room, knowing they can't hear you since it's soundproof but wanting to be close anyway."

"I know they want to be here, but I can't make them watch this. And I don't know if I want them to. Does that make me a bad person?"

Max was the one who answered. "No, it doesn't. They each had their own issues and personal fights. And you're going to have your own right now. I'll be here. As will your new family. The girls are right outside, and they'll be the ones to help you heal, and probably help with your first shift when the time comes and the new moon comes out. But don't worry, we're going to be here."

Her mate might have been the one to tell her not to

worry, but she knew he was worrying more than the rest. Because he could feel her pain in the moments she was used as a Conduit for the artifact. At least he experienced her reaction to it. She wasn't sure anyone could feel the power funneling through her system. She did not want to die because she wasn't strong enough to stop Blade.

And she didn't want to die because she wasn't strong enough to take Gideon's bite.

She had taken Max's bite on her shoulder, and that had been the most pleasurable experience of her life. This was going to be something completely different, and she was well aware of that.

But she would survive it, damn it. Even if she had to swallow back a little bile along the way.

"Let's get this over with. Because the more that I stand here, the more I get nervous, and the more I think about every single physiological thing that I can. That's the hard part about being a vet. I might not be a complete doctor like you, but I still have those letters behind my name, and I still took a lot of the same classes. So, I really don't want to think about exactly where Gideon's going to have to bite, and exactly what's going to happen at a medical level. So, let's just quickly get some biting done, and then I'll be a shifter. Right?"

She knew she was talking quickly and like she was going insane, but the fear was starting to take over. Max must have realized that because he reached out, touched her face with his hand, and kissed her softly. Then, all she could think about was him and his taste and everything that she would miss out on if she didn't survive this.

She wanted to know everything else that there was to know when it came to him and what they could be.

So, she would survive this.

Damn it. She was going to survive.

Walker and Leah helped chain her up, while Max whispered to her and told her stories about when he was a pup. She knew the others could hear, but since all of them except Leah had actually been there during that time, she knew Max didn't mind. He told her stories of the time when he had fallen into a puddle and gotten completely muddy, and because Mitchell had been close and completely clean, Max had shaken his entire little body as quickly as he could and ended up getting mud on both of them. His mother had not been pleased but had laughed as she cleaned them both up.

Those were the childhood stories Cheyenne needed to hear, not just the ones that made her cry.

And she wanted more of those tales, she needed more memories they made together. She wanted to make sure that that little pup named Mark healed completely and could grow up in a world where he wasn't afraid to be who he was or terrified because he wasn't Blade's Pack.

And those thoughts, along with myriad others, helped Cheyenne to kiss Max one last time and tell him goodbye.

Not goodbye forever, but "see you later" so he could get on the other side of the room and get behind Parker and Brandon and the others. They needed to hold him back because this was going to hurt.

They chained her down, but they were softer chains surrounded by leather and cotton. They had explained to her that she needed to remain in the exact same position so Gideon didn't make a mistake. Because he had to be close to his wolf in order for this to happen. He needed to be the most dominant he could be to make sure there was no mistake when it came to the change.

He would have to be connected to his animal, and, as a vet, Cheyenne knew what happened when animals' senses got heightened, they went a little insane. But then she remembered that this was paranormal, this was magic. She would be okay.

She wasn't going to die.

Not today. She let out a breath, met Max's eyes, and then closed her own. She didn't want to see his face when she screamed.

Because she was going to scream.

Gideon started the process of changing into his wolf while she was being put onto the rack. It took a while for most wolves to shift. Sometimes, it took as long as ten minutes for the new ones. It was a painful process, and she could hear the sounds of bones popping and muscles tearing, tendons rending. But soon, he was a large wolf, and she could feel his breath on her skin.

The first bite was fire in her veins.

The second was worse.

The third drew her into an abyss of flame and torture.

And then there was the fourth. And a fifth. And then...there was screaming.

And not just hers. Max howled, she would know the sound anywhere.

The others joined in with him, a haunting melody of beauty and terror.

But for some reason, it gave Cheyenne strength.

Because she would survive for Max. She was going to survive for them.

And then Gideon bit again, but she didn't feel anything.

She only felt Max.

When she woke up, Cheyenne was back in the clinic room she had been in after Blade's attack. Max once again sat by her side, and a blanket covered her. She didn't have a single wound on her.

Max was on his feet as soon as she opened his eyes, as if he had been waiting for her and listening for the barest sound of movement.

"You're awake." He lowered his head and brushed his lips on hers, a gentle caress that she barely felt. She wanted more but was afraid it might be a little too much right then.

"I am." She paused as she felt something inside of her, something pushing through. She couldn't breathe, couldn't think. "Max, I need to go outside. I think...I think some-thing's inside me. I think I need to shift."

She clawed at her skin, her heart beating fast. Sweat broke out on her body, and her flesh went clammy. Max's eyes widened, and he shoved down the blanket to pull her up.

"That's not supposed to happen for another week, at least, Cheyenne. You're not supposed to shift the same day you get bit. But, Jesus, it's not like the two of us are normal. Come on. Come on. It might just be a reaction to the Healing, or it could be whatever Blade is doing. Either way, I'm going to get you outside. I'm going to help you shift if that's what's about to happen. But I'm going to make sure Walker is here."

Cheyenne held back a scream as something inside her *pushed*. She didn't know what it was or why she felt this way, but she *knew* it was her wolf.

As Max had said...

The two of them were anything but ordinary.

Soon, Max had her on the grass outside of the clinic and started pulling off her clothes. She heard footsteps as Walker ran toward them, his hands out as if he needed to Heal.

But she couldn't focus on either of them, only on what was happening to her.

Her bones broke, her body changing shape as if it were always meant to do this. Her face elongated, and her teeth grew into fangs. White fur sprouted through her skin before sinking back in and coming out again.

And throughout it all, she didn't feel any pain.

She should be feeling pain.

You will next time. This is my gift.

She knew that was the voice of the moon goddess. It had to be.

This was the deity's gift.

And Cheyenne was now a wolf.

She was a shifter.

She was Pack.

And as she stood on all fours next to Max and Walker on their knees, she knew her life had altered once more. She wasn't the woman looking in any longer. An outsider no more.

She was the Conduit. She was a Talon. She was Max's mate.

And now...now, she was wolf.

BLADE

One more time.

One more time, and then he'd be ready for the next phase.

One more try.

Blade looked down at the artifact in his hand and knew that he would have to take out Cheyenne before he completed the final task. But for now, he could make one more stand.

He'd take out one more Alpha.

Gain one more step in his rule as the Supreme Alpha.

And then he'd reign over them all.

CHAPTER FOURTEEN

Cheyenne ducked from the fist coming at her face and almost smiled before she remembered that she was supposed to keep her attention on the fight and not on the fact that she'd successfully dodged a punch.

She moved again as Aimee's jab came for her once more, and this time, it connected with her shoulder. Cheyenne winced, rubbing out the sting, then grinned as her friend did a little booty dance.

This is the first time they were sparring together for training, although each of them had been fighting with others up until this point. They were going on two weeks of learning to use their new abilities. Well, Cheyenne's new skills since Aimee had been a shifter for longer.

But Cheyenne was doing better, at least she was *trying* to do better.

The others told her that she had shifted far faster than anyone they'd ever heard of. That should have worried her, but there were so many other things to worry about, she could only focus on getting better and not being a liability. Gideon and Max had both told her that everything was probably due to her being connected to the artifact. Though it wasn't like they knew all of the details when it came to the stone that had changed everything.

Aimee stopped her dance and opened her arms. Cheyenne hugged her friend close and kissed her temple. It was so weird, this new life of hers, but she was finding her way. The fact that she and Aimee were training in fighting and learning how to use their bodies as weapons while learning how to control their beasts was insane. It felt like, one moment, Cheyenne was helping animals. The next, she had claws and fangs just like one.

Not that Cheyenne wanted to call herself an animal, nor would she call any of her Packmates that, but the vet jokes hadn't stopped, even with the underlying tension within the Pack.

In the weeks since she had shifted, there hadn't been a single incident with Blade. In fact, the entire Aspen Pack was closed up. No one went in, no one came out. Both the Talons and the Redwoods were watching. The European Pack was also watching and had secretly sent over a few of their wolves over time. Cheyenne hadn't met any of them yet since they hadn't wanted to stay within the Talon den, but Max had told her they were near. Everyone was gearing up for a battle that seemed to be on the horizon, even if she couldn't quite see it.

Because Blade was testing everyone. That's what all of these siphons of energy were. It had to be.

He was slowly killing off those he thought weakest—though she didn't know exactly why—and showing every single Alpha he could that he could have their power with the snap of his fingers.

She didn't think Blade knew or planned on all of the energy flowing through her. If he did know, she was afraid that she'd become just another target for him.

What would he do to her? Attack the den? That already seemed like a given.

"Again?" Aimee asked, bringing Cheyenne out of her thoughts of war and demise.

"Sure. I think I'm punching too early, I don't have control of my senses yet."

Everything was heightened now that she'd become a wolf. Max had said she would learn how to deal with that over time, but sometimes, things were a little too loud, or she could smell something from far away. Just the night before, they had been making eggs, and she'd had to stop because the smell was too much for her. Max had nodded, taking care of it, and then helped her to relax so she could get a hold of her senses. Everything had changed, including what she could eat. Some things tasted a little too sharp, a little too salty. And she couldn't even drink her way out of all the stress because her new metabolism burned through alcohol way too quickly.

Max and the rest of his brothers and cousins drank beer, but it was apparently just for show and for the taste. They couldn't actually get drunk unless they drank a lot. That happened, and she knew from Max that he had tried a few times to get completely toasted after losing his arm, but he hadn't done that in a while.

In fact, as she watched him fight with Kameron across the way, she knew that he was just as comfortable with himself now as he likely was before. He battled with grace and an intelligence that spoke of skill and instinct. Kameron was slightly faster, but since he was the Enforcer, Cheyenne expected that.

Max was beautiful when he fought. He helped her at home, as well, teaching her some of the techniques he knew. Because she was smaller, though, she liked learning from some of the female lieutenants. Kameron's men and women trained daily, even if they didn't have to spar for hours every day sometimes. But the women that worked for Kameron and the rest of the Pack had been able to show Cheyenne what to do with her body since her center of gravity was a little bit lower than the rest of them.

Aimee and Cheyenne went back to fighting, pausing only when Kameron and Max came over to give them some tips.

If Cheyenne wasn't studying to figure out if they could find anything on the artifact, something that was becoming less and less likely as time moved on, she was finding ways to strengthen her connection to her wolf and her skills. She should be exhausted, and if she were still human, she knew she would have been passed out early every night.

But she wasn't. She could sense her wolf within her, but Cheyenne wasn't sure what she felt about the other soul inside her body. Her wolf felt the same and that was an odd thought. But the fact that her wolf was there at all kept her energy up. After trying to find her place, Cheyenne came home and just spent time with Max. She wanted to learn who he was, and she would try to make sure he knew who she was.

But at the same time, she knew they were both changing. Neither of them was the same person they were before. But wasn't that the point of falling? Wasn't that the point of creating a mating bond?

Maybe if she were still human, or if she had fallen for a man who wasn't a shifter, things would be different. Cheyenne had gone on dates before Max and had been in some serious relationships before. But she'd never truly fallen in love. Enough time had now passed that maybe if either of them were still human, they could have felt this on their own. But the mating bond pulsated between them every day, and it just increased what they felt for each other, ramping it up at such a rapid pace that, sometimes, she felt as if she were struggling to catch up.

But then she looked at Max, saw the way he cared for

his family and put his all into trying to save his Pack—and her for that matter—and she knew that what she was feeling wasn't wrong.

It just wasn't human.

But she wasn't human anymore either.

Max came up from behind her and put his hand on her hip. She looked up at him, raising her brow, and he rolled his eyes. The fact that he did that, something he wouldn't have done when they first met, made her warm inside. He was beginning to come into his own, starting to be the Max that people missed. But throughout it all, he was still her Max. And that counted for everything.

"You're reacting too early because you're anticipating what she's going to do. And because you two are best friends, you happen to know what she's going to do. And it helps that you were both trained by the same people. But if you're going to be on a battlefield with another wolf from another Pack, they're not going to fight the same as Aimee. So, you're not going to be able to anticipate what they'll do the same way. I still want you to anticipate what they're doing by watching their movements rather than what you think they'll do in any given situation, though." She met Max's gaze and nodded.

"That makes sense."

"So, why don't you do it again, but this time, with me?" Max winked, and she grinned. She knew that the others were watching, noticing the way Max smiled more, how he actually laughed out loud. He hadn't laughed before, not with her. And she knew that the Max she saw now was the Max he would become, rather than the two separate versions he had been in the past. He was healing, and maybe that was partly due to her, but she didn't think so. People were asking him questions, coming to him for answers. And he was finding his place within the Pack.

And that counted for something.

She was just about to duck again because Max was fast when she fell to her knees. Everyone stopped moving around them, and she heard rumblings of people afraid that Max had actually hit her. But he hadn't made contact.

Instead, it was something far worse.

She looked up at her mate, her eyes wide. "The artifact. He's trying to use the artifact."

KAMERON CALLED FOR WALKER. Cheyenne could hear him yelling it as well as using his phone. Walker must have been close but not within hearing range.

"I'm here, Cheyenne. Tell me what to do." Max was on his knees in front of her, cupping her face. She leaned into his hand, taking in his strength not only from his presence but also through their bond. "Just pull through. You're strong, Cheyenne. So damn strong."

"I'm going to. I'm going to try to...try to, I don't know, put the energy back. Or just stop him. I'm stronger now. I can feel it." She screamed, unable to hold back the pain, and Max pulled her against his chest.

"Don't do anything that will kill you. Or even hurt you. Because I'm going to get really fucking pissed off if you hurt my mate."

She snorted at that and then writhed in pain. It felt like her entire body was being ripped through a tiny pinprick hole and then shoved back through it. But she could feel the energy, and if she closed her eyes, focused, and used the steadying presence of her mate and her best friends around her, she could concentrate. She knew that Dawn, Dhani, and Aimee were there. Walker and Leah were there, as well. Almost everyone she cared about was around, making sure that she had strength.

And those that weren't there were out protecting the Pack and the den itself.

The Talons were strong. And that meant Cheyenne had to be stronger.

So she closed her eyes even tighter and focused on the energy pooling within her and that which was being siphoned out. It didn't feel like the same bond she had with Max. That was like a cord, one that she could almost mentally grab and tug. And every time she did, she felt his emotions. Felt, dare she say it, his love.

So, she wrapped herself around that, protected it. It was almost as if she put a coating on it, making sure that nothing could touch it. It was the most important thing within her.

And then she looked back at the artifact's energy, wrapped her metaphysical hands around it, and pushed.

She swore she heard a scream on the other end of her consciousness, and she knew it had nothing to do with Max or her. That was all Blade. Something she had done had hurt him, but it wasn't enough.

So she shoved again, this time, towards the origin of the power, the one who should have been holding that lifeforce, that Alpha-ness. She pushed and pushed, putting all of her strength into that. She knew she was screaming, knew she was gasping for breath. There was sweat pouring down her face, and the others were mumbling around her, but she had no idea what they were saying.

Instead, she focused on that energy and pushed again.

And then it was almost as if a fuse blew, and she screamed again, thrown back into Max as the power went away. She didn't know if someone had died or if she had beaten Blade in this tiny, little battle.

But she had done *something*.

Cheyenne opened her eyes to see Walker above her, his hands outstretched. He was Healing her, and she knew she was once again bleeding from her nose and ears and eyes. "Is it as bad as before?" she asked, her voice a rasp. "No, it's just different," Walker said. "You're going to be fine."

"You're not going to be fine once I beat your ass for doing that," Max grumbled. But it didn't sound like he actually meant it. He was just scared, and honestly, so was she. They had talked about what it meant to be a Conduit, and she hadn't known that she could do what she just did until she'd done it. There was no practicing when it came to what was going on with her.

So she let Walker and then Leah help her because she felt helpless. Perhaps she had done something, or maybe she had made it worse, there was just no telling.

By the time the others were done, Max had picked her up and carried her to their house. She didn't think about it as *his* house anymore, it was theirs.

He sat her in bed and tucked the blankets around her even though she still wore her clothes. She hadn't bled on her own clothing, only Max's, so now he was shirtless, running around trying to take care of her. She couldn't help but lick her lips at the sight of him.

With all the new energy running through her thanks to the Healing, she wasn't tired. But she would let Max take care of her. If it made him happy, she could do that.

Yet what she really wanted was to be near him, to touch him.

"You can't do that again," Max said as he got into bed with her. "Gideon just called, and one of the Packs from Florida said their Alpha lost his power for maybe a minute before it slammed back into him. And this time, only one wolf died. Another wolf was on the way, and then suddenly, he was able to break from whatever was happening to him. That was you, Cheyenne. You did that."

She closed her eyes, letting out a breath. "I wish I could have done more. I just hate feeling helpless."

"You're anything but helpless, Cheyenne. I remember

when I first came out of the clinic after the battle with the humans, wondering if I should be dead. I thought I knew what helpless meant. I had to figure out how to do even normal things differently. Countless people in the world are either born or, through some chance of fate, have to learn to live with only one arm, but I'd never really heard of a wolf that had to deal with that. We heal so quickly, it's almost unheard of. It just took me a long time to figure out exactly what I was supposed to do, and how to fit in again. Finding myself so close to death like that? I didn't like who I was, and I knew I couldn't go back to who I had been. And every time I tried to move a step forward, I just looked at my family and how much they were growing, and I felt helpless."

"You're anything but helpless, Max," Cheyenne said, repeating his words. She snuggled into him, inhaling his scent. Now that she could smell so much more, she knew she would never forget the essence of Max. She was his, and she knew his scent was embedded in her pores, just like hers was in his.

"I'm just glad you're here," she said, her voice soft. "I'm just happy I'm with you. And I shouldn't be happy, not right now, not with everything going on. But you make me happy. I couldn't do any of this without you."

"And you know I couldn't do anything without you. I think we make each other stronger. Don't you think?" He leaned forward and kissed her. "I love you, Cheyenne. I love everything about you. I love the fact that I fell for you before I should have. I love that you fight for anything you feel is an injustice. I love the fact that you helped me discover exactly who I was all along rather than the person I thought I had to hide from."

Cheyenne's eyes filled with tears, and she kissed him back. "I love you, too. I love you with everything that I am. You surprised me, Max Brentwood. I never thought I would have this, never thought I would have you, and I don't want to lose you."

"Then don't do anything stupid. Don't sacrifice yourself. Let us find another way."

There was so much hurt, so much pain in his voice, that she had to move around so she could kiss him harder. "As long as you don't do anything stupid either, Max."

"You're mine," he said softly. "Always."

"Always," she whispered.

Just like you're mine.

She didn't say it.

But he knew it.

No matter what happened next, she knew they would be together.

They had to be.

CHAPTER FIFTEEN

"You look like you haven't slept in days," Mitchell said, pulling Max out of his thoughts.

Max hadn't even realized he was so focused on himself again instead of on the fact that Mitchell had invited him over for a little brother time. Things had been heating up, and Max knew it would probably only get worse.

There hadn't been any skirmishes or even bombings like there was with the humans, and there hadn't been any more deaths since Cheyenne fought back against Blade.

This was such a weird battle strategy for the Talons, though, and Max knew that Gideon and the rest were feeling like they were at their wits' end.

The Talons couldn't fight back with claws or fangs if there wasn't anyone to fight against. The Aspens were so closed-in, and they hadn't heard from Audrey. Max feared the worst with that.

The Aspen Beta had helped them and had possibly sacrificed her life to do so.

"There you go again," Mitchell said calmly, and Max blinked. "What the hell are you thinking about over there?"

"Just the fact that we're fighting an unseen force. Blade keeps coming at us and is literally killing people, and there's nothing we can do."

"I know. Do you think I like this? I feel like I'm sitting on my fucking hands instead of being able to do anything for anybody. All I can do is watch your mate almost die over and over again as she tries to do something. But what can she do? What can any of us do? We can't get into the Aspen den, and it looks like we're just going to have to wait for Blade to make the next move, that doesn't include the shady tricks that he's been up to."

"You know it's a sad day when you almost miss a human government with a tank and a witch on the edge. It was easier to fight when we knew what was coming at us."

"But did we know what was coming at us? It's always been scary, always been one thing after another. One new thing after another. It's never been just wolf on wolf. At least not for a few years."

"And do we even want that? I just want peace. I just

want my mate out of the line of fire. And that's all she seems to be in these days."

"You're telling me. Blade was the one who thought Dawn would be the perfect sacrifice in order to show us that the Centrals didn't need to be a Pack and they deserved to die. Blade took my mate, and she almost died. And then Aimee almost died. And then Dhani almost died. We lost wolves, we lost friends. And all because Blade is an egomaniac that we just can't take out."

"We'll get him. Because I don't think we're going to have another choice."

Mitchell sighed and pinched the bridge of his nose. Max's brother was Beta, and that meant, at least in the Talon Pack, that Mitchell was responsible for the needs of every single Pack member. The Enforcer did the protecting, the Omega dealt with emotions, the Healer handled physical injuries, and the Alpha took care of everything else. But the Beta and the Heir, Ryder, were the ones that brought it all together. And that meant that Max was on the outside looking in. He was always there to help, but without those extra bonds, there wasn't much he could do without being ordered to do it. He tried to do more and even put himself out there more than he used to over the years, but sometimes, being the one without a title took its toll.

Or at least it had.

He'd slowly found his way and his place. Yes, it had taken losing part of himself and then finding it again with

Cheyenne, but here he was, ready to fight. Prepared to be who he needed to be. "You know, Mitchell, I know you guys worry about me. And I guess I gave you need to worry."

"We thought you were going to die. And not just on that battlefield." Mitchell paused, and Max knew his brother was remembering everything that had happened back when they finished fighting the humans. "You almost died. And then when Walker said you would be fine and we would find a way to make sure that you could be the way you were, you closed yourself off from us. I thought we'd lost you forever. You didn't smile anymore. You didn't lean down and kiss the women's cheeks anymore. Remember when you did that to one of the newly mated? I thought her mate was going to rip your face off."

Mitchell smiled as he said it, and that brought a smile to Max's face. "I used to be happier. But maybe that was because you shielded me for so long."

Mitchell shook his head. "I never shielded you. Not enough. You dealt with your own shit. Dad beat the shit out of you, just like he did me. You saw the others die, saw the weakest die. You saw our mother die because Dad was an asshole. You were there for all of it. So I can't say that I shielded you. But I *can* say that you were the one who faced it all and said you were going to find the good in it. That you were going to be the person you wanted to be, rather than one forged in flame."

"And yet I ended up being that man anyway."

"I don't think you're the man forged in flames. You're the man you needed to be after everything happened. And I guess it took me a long time to realize that. I thought I had failed you, Max. Because I couldn't save you that day. Walker could, and so could the others who held your body together. But I wasn't there to push that man out of the way. And I think I should have. It doesn't make rational sense, but you're my baby brother. And I'm the big brother. That's sort of what I do."

"I don't think that I'm the right man to say this, and maybe that's because I always feel like I'm one step behind, but I think that whatever happened needed to happen. I used to believe in fate more than I do now. And I used to look fate in the face and say that everything happened for a reason. And then when it did happen, when the worst happened—at least the worst at the time —I thought maybe it happened because I wasn't good enough. Because fate decided a Brentwood needed to die, or at least lose part of himself. And I was the one who was most easily lost. After all, I wasn't the one that was going to break bonds when I died. There would be no shifting in the power structure when the Pack lost me."

"That's insane." Mitchell growled out the words, and Max figured that his brother was about to leap off the couch at any moment and beat the shit out of him.

Max held up his hand and shook his head. "Stop. I had those thoughts, and I can't help it. Because sometimes when you look at all the amazing things that you and the rest of the family have done for this Pack and our people? It's hard to live up to it. And I know you don't mean to make me feel that way. That's on me. And I know you all have your own burdens. Believe me, I know you do. But, sometimes, it's just hard to not be able to help the way I want to. And, yes, that's selfish of me. And that's something I have to deal with on my own. I don't know if it bothered me as much before the attack, but when I was already so vulnerable physically, and even mentally after what happened, those thoughts seeped in and tugged at me. But I'm not that man anymore."

"Because of Cheyenne?"

"Yes, and no. She was a surprise."

"A hell of a surprise."

"I don't know who I would have been without her. But I also don't know who she would have been without me. And maybe that's egotistical, but isn't that what mates are supposed to do? They're not supposed to change for each other, but *with* each other. I always looked at her and wondered what could have been. But my wolf didn't feel her, and maybe that's because the moon goddess didn't decide we should be mates until the last moment. Or maybe it was because I was broken inside. Or I just hid from anything that could have been my future because I was scared. I don't know, but that's not really something I can ask. The moon goddess doesn't talk to me, she just shows up and scares the hell out of all of us."

"Tell me about it. But I'm happy for you, Max. You and

Cheyenne keep saying that things have moved fast, but have they? You were both thrown into this situation where you're always crossing paths, always in each other's spheres. And, remember, we're not human. Mating happens for a reason, and I would know that."

Considering his brother's past, Max knew that was a hard statement to even say.

"But back to what I was saying before. I don't feel like I'm left behind anymore. I don't feel like I have to work harder to prove who I am. So maybe I'm healing, or maybe I'm just becoming the Max that I need to be now. But I don't think I need a true connection to the hierarchy anymore to feel like I'm the person I need to be. If that were to ever happen, by the way, I'd do my best. But in order for that to happen, one of you guys has to give up your bonds, and that's not something I want to think about."

"Uh, yeah, let's not even think about that."

"And now I need to head over to my mate, because we have a little more studying to do before I can finally tell her that it's time for bed."

Mitchell laughed and shook his head then stood up and brought Max into a big hug. Max leaned into his brother, inhaling the scent that always reminded him of home. His parents hadn't been the best people. His mother had been weak, unable to protect them even though sometimes he thought she wanted to. But through all their horrors, Max always had his brother. Yes, he had his cousins, too, but his brother was different. And Max knew his cousins felt the same way about each other.

"Go tell your mate that we're thinking of her and we're going to figure out a way to disconnect her from the artifact before we destroy it. I hope you know that."

Max nodded, his fists clenched by his sides. "I'm not going to lose her, Mitchell. I just found her. And even if she wasn't my mate... Let's pretend that this has nothing to do with me and I'm not the center of this universe right now."

Mitchell laughed, and Max smiled.

"No matter what, I'm not going to let her die. She deserves a happy and full life. She deserves to grow with her friends and figure out exactly who she is in this new world. She deserves everything, and I'm going to do all in my power to make sure that happens."

"Out of all of us, Max? I think you're the one who can do that."

Max hugged his brother again and then headed over to his house where Cheyenne was, books strewn across the coffee table. His mate was stalking the kitchen, pacing back and forth. There was a tension in the air that worried him, and he frowned. He moved a few steps closer, and she turned. Her eyes were wide, bloodshot, and tears streamed down her cheeks.

"What?"

"Xavier found something. In one of the books."

"What did he find?" Max tried to sound calm, but it

was hard when he knew that whatever she was about to read to him, whatever she was going to show him, wouldn't be good. She walked over to him and to the book that lay on the island in front of them.

"Here. You should read it."

"Come here. Let me hold you."

She sank into his side, and he wrapped his arm around her as he looked down at the book in front of him. The blood in his veins grew cold, and his jaw tightened. His wolf howled, clawing at the edges of his skin, wanting out, wanting retribution that would never come.

"This is wrong. We're going to find another way."

"You know what it says. In order to fully take out the artifact and make sure the moon goddess has it in her hold, those connected to it must end. And that's Blade."

A pause. "And me."

"No. That's not going to happen. I'm not going to lose you. You're not going to lose either."

"I don't think we have a choice, Max. I think that whatever happens, we're going to have to face it head-on. But I'm not going to let everyone die around me so I can have a chance. Because in the end, I might die anyway."

"No." He cupped her face and kissed her hard.

"What if we don't have a choice?"

"There's always a choice. That's what I've learned after so many years living in this Pack. There's always a choice."

"A choice? I want that to be true. But what if it's not? Max? Make love to me. Just make me forget. Give me tonight. Tomorrow, we can find the answers. Just give me tonight."

And because he couldn't find the words, he kissed his mate and picked her up, setting her ass on the counter.

"Tonight."

Tomorrow, they would find the answers. Tomorrow, they would save the world and maybe themselves.

Tonight, he would make sure his mate knew she was loved. And that she was his.

He kissed her softly, loving her taste, wanting more. She tugged on his shirt, and he lifted his arms, allowing her to remove it. Then his mouth was back on her, tasting her, craving her.

Her hands roamed up and down his back, and she growled. He couldn't help but smirk, his cock pressing against his jeans as she ran her fingernails down his back. They weren't claws yet since she was still so new, but it was close enough. His mate was all wolf, and he loved her more than anything.

He didn't have to hold back now, though tonight would be soft, just the two of them.

Later, they would let their wolves out to play.

He quickly divested her of her shirt before leaning down to lick her nipples. He loved the fact that she hadn't worn a bra, and secretly knew it was for him. She loved when he sucked on her nipples and liked giving him easy access when they were at home.

He tried to push out all the thoughts that threatened

to overwhelm him at the idea of what would happen next. But for now, he could at least focus on his mate and what they meant to each other.

"Max. I need you in me."

"I can do that," he growled, then stripped her out of the rest of her clothes, tearing them when they got in his way, and tossing them around the kitchen.

She pulled at his pants, but before she could undo the button, he went to his knees and started licking at her pussy. He loved eating her out, loved the little noises she made when he hit just the right spot. He especially loved the fact that his beard scraped her just enough to leave her aching for more, her inner thighs so soft it was all he could do not to bite and taste.

"Max!" she came on his face, one leg hanging over his shoulder, the other foot planted on him for support.

Then he had his pants down below his ass and was inside her, her aching heat already clenching around him from her previous orgasm. He had to hold back a groan and bite his tongue so he wouldn't come right then. It was so damn hard when she was this hot and always so close to sending him over the edge.

"You're so tight for me. Always so warm and perfect."

She grinned up at him, wrapping her legs around his waist and her arms around his shoulders. "I can say the same about you and that mighty dick of yours."

He snorted, even as he pumped inside of her. Only

with Cheyenne could he feel so much at once. "Mighty dick?"

"We can name it later, but for now, fuck me, Max Brentwood. Make love to me. Make me yours."

So he did, moving fast, moving hard, even if he was still more gentle with her than he would have been at any other time. He was afraid as soon as he let go, they'd have to face their reality and the battle coming.

He couldn't, though. Couldn't look forward when all he wanted to do was look at his mate.

She must have known what he was thinking because she brought her lips to his and kissed him with every ounce of...*everything* she had.

So he pumped harder, needing more. He slid his hand between them and brushed his thumb over her clit.

And then she came, right on his shaft, and he filled her up, not stopping his movements until he was wrung dry, and she was holding onto him as if she couldn't keep herself up.

He held her close, toed out of his pants, then carried her naked to their bathroom. He'd give her a bath and hold her for the rest of the night.

And in the morning, they'd face what they needed to, together.

Tonight, though, tonight...they could forget.

Tonight would be about them.

Because tonight may be the last.

He just hoped to the goddess it wasn't.

AUDREY

Audrey wasn't dead, but sometimes she sure felt like it. She looked down at her raw and bleeding wrists and hoped to hell she'd start healing soon. It wasn't like she could go to her Healer, not now, not when she was on the run from her Pack, her own Alpha.

She'd always known there was something off about Blade, but she'd thought it was because he was a misogynistic asshole who hadn't like the fact that a woman had been blessed by the moon goddess as his Beta.

She'd gotten used to the barbs.

The innuendoes.

And she's fought off every challenger who had dared come at her, thinking they could show their strength to their Alpha and the goddess.

Audrey had won those challenges and had done her

best to do it with a fierce grace that would hopefully show the others that she was strong physically and emotionally.

The dynamics and balance of being a female Beta who also happened to be a lion shifter wasn't for the timid.

But she'd done it.

And then Blade had gotten worse. He'd shown his true side. And she'd honestly tried to save her Pack. She'd thought she found a way to make sure Blade didn't ruin everything, that he didn't destroy the Pack from within because of his greed.

But he'd given her orders to stay away, commands her lion had been forced to obey even as the human rebelled. That was why he was Alpha, and she was Beta.

He was just strong enough that it broke parts of her deep inside to disobey him. And though she'd tried, she hadn't been able to, not really. She hadn't been able to tell those who needed to know the truth anything until it was far too late.

She'd saved that young woman from the Talon Pack, and in doing so, had broken a law in her Pack so taboo that she hadn't been able to hide it from her Alpha. She might have tried to fight back, but he had others on his side, those who thought individuals weaker or different than they were should be culled from this Earth.

Audrey had known the only reason Blade and the others tolerated her kind or the others hiding within the den, was because Blade liked knowing he held a secret, and thereby had power when it came to those still hidden from not only the humans but also the other shifters and magic users in other Packs.

When she came back to the Aspen den after helping Aimee, Blade had been waiting. She hadn't been able to fight off the other wolves and hadn't seen the sun or the moon since.

He'd caged her. He'd chained her.

He treated her like his pet.

But the last time he'd come to beat her and whip her, he'd looked weaker than he ever had before.

Audrey withstood each blow because she knew she'd get out of this. She would fight for her Pack and for those who needed her help. She'd gone through worse, and she'd be damned if this Alpha would win.

But he hadn't looked like the Blade who had captured her.

And when he left, his body grey and weak, he'd left the cage open. He'd forgotten, and he never let anyone near her other than himself, so the entire place smelled only of him and her fear.

Only it wasn't fear anymore.

It was hope.

She'd found her way out of the cage and the basement he'd held her in. She'd always been able to get out of the locks, that had never been the problem. The problem was the cage and the shackles themselves. Blade's witch had cursed them before she died. But it had simply taken Blade's lack of thought for Audrey to get out.

She found an old dresser full of clothes for the shifters on call and pulled on a pair of jeans and a shirt that happened to fit, thankful there were also reasonably fitting boots in the closet. She didn't know who she was stealing from as the whole place reeked of more than a few shifters, but she was grateful that she had something to wear other than the rags she'd been wearing. She still smelled and needed to wash her hair badly, but she'd do that later.

Soon after, she found one of the offices Blade used to make his plans and snatched one of the folders on a high stack. She didn't know what was in it, but if it could help, she'd use it. Then she was out of the den, running away from those who needed her.

She couldn't help her people if she was dead.

Now, she was covered in sweat but free. At least as free as she could be still connected to Blade and the Aspens through her bonds. She shut them down as much as she could so no one could find her if they looked, but it hurt to do so. She couldn't break the bonds completely, not when she had those she loved and cared for back in the den.

She'd come back for them. That much she promised herself.

And when she opened the folder, having waited because she didn't want to look down and see a menu or something equally as worthless, her heart nearly stopped.

Tears filled her eyes, and she blinked them away.

This could help the Talons and the others. She knew they were fighting back because Blade was always angrier than ever after they defeated him.

Blade was going to lure them out to a battlefield soon, using the weakest of the Aspens as bait. That made Audrey's skin crawl, but she did her best not to growl and alert anyone nearby that she was hiding up in the trees. She was a cat, after all, that was where she felt the safest.

Blade would be at a specific place at a specific time in two days.

If she could get to the Talons and warn them, they could catch Blade unaware.

This could help. It had to help. All she'd gone through could *not* be in vain.

She just prayed to the moon goddess that she wasn't too late.

CHAPTER SIXTEEN

Cheyenne knew they had an advantage, she just hoped it was enough. Audrey had been a blessing. A frail, bleeding, and clearly hurt blessing, who held so much anger within her, Cheyenne was afraid the woman would break at the slightest stress.

But Audrey was strong, that much was clear.

And Cheyenne knew that she had to be just as strong.

There was no other choice.

When Audrey came, she'd brought maps and details about Blade's plan. After everything that had happened, after every failure and inability to find exactly what they needed to do to survive, this was like a gift from the goddess herself.

And maybe it was.

As soon as they made sure that Audrey was well enough to make it through the night, they had contacted the Redwood Pack, the Central Pack, the Coven, and the Thames Pack. Allister, as well as a few of his men, were actually already in the United States. Cheyenne hadn't been aware that Allister himself had come when she heard that some of the Thames members had entered the den, but in retrospect, it made sense.

For the Alpha to leave his den, that meant he was ready to fight, ready to sacrifice everything to protect his people.

She knew the other Alphas, as well as the Coven leader, would do the same. Because they planned to meet Blade before he was ready. Apparently, Blade was going to use the artifact on the battlefield to draw them in.

Well, they were already on their way.

Before he could use the magic.

Before he was ready.

And, hopefully, that would be enough. With any luck, that would give them enough time.

Parker and Gideon had even done the nearly unimaginable and had contacted the US government. The humans would be on the battlefield with them—not fighting them this time, but fighting alongside them. Gideon would be in charge, the point-man for the whole event. It had been eighteen hours of no sleep, and adrenaline ran through all of them. But now, they were ready.

Humans, wolves, multiple Packs, and witches alike fighting against a common enemy.

One that was strong because of his people and because of the dark magic he used.

As long as Blade didn't find a way to use the artifact on everyone at once, they could beat him.

At least, that was the hope.

"Cheyenne? Are you okay?" Max came up to her and tugged on her bulletproof vest. She wouldn't be shifting today because the only reason she was out on the battlefield at all, or at least planning to be out on the battlefield, was because she needed to be close just in case she could figure out how to stop Blade from using the artifact. She'd almost done it once, had even saved someone because of it. And if she trained hard enough, or at least focused hard enough, she might be able to do it again.

That meant she got to wear a bulletproof vest, because while the humans would definitely be using weapons, and wolves usually just used fangs and claws, they weren't sure what Blade would do. The rules of engagement were far different than they used to be, and they weren't taking any chances.

Namely, Max wasn't taking any chances with her.

"I'm fine. Just oddly wanting to get this over with, and worried about the fact that it's actually here all at the same time."

He kissed her forehead then her lips. People mulled about all around them, getting ready to attack, and doing whatever they needed to do before they started fighting.

They were near where the clearing was located, but

thanks to the witches from the Coven and the Packs themselves, they were hidden from view using temporary wards. No one would be able to see them, not even the satellites from the human governments.

Two squadrons of humans would fight alongside the group, and there were others waiting in the wings, and even more standing by to see what would happen if Blade prevailed.

Because if the Packs lost, then the end of humanity as they knew it would likely be over.

It was a daunting revelation, but one they all understood. They would fight against Blade, all of them as one. But first, Cheyenne knew she had to try and stop the artifact itself. Because if she didn't, then there was no hope.

Just a bit of responsibility on her shoulders. She bit her tongue so she couldn't say it. She didn't want to die today, but both she and Max knew she might. She had just found the man she loved, had only now found a way to be with her friends and new family until the end of days. But it seemed her end might be today. It wasn't fair, but life wasn't fair. It didn't matter how many years someone lived, sometimes, life just wasn't fair.

It hadn't been fair to Dawn that she had to grow up in a Pack that had to hide from the others because of what had happened to her forebears. It hadn't been fair to Aimee that she was made to live her life knowing she was dying because of a curse that had happened years before she was born. It hadn't been fair to Dhani that she grew up knowing that something was different about her, but had to find out that she'd been stripped of her powers because her grandmother was forced to bind them to save Dhani's life.

It hadn't been fair to her friends, and yet they survived.

Cheyenne just hoped that, somehow, she'd be able to find a way to survive.

"You're starting to scare me, Cheyenne. You're not saying anything."

She swallowed hard before she spoke. "I know I'm going to have to close the Conduit today. This is the last step. This is where Blade has all his plans laid out, where he intends to kill everybody in his path. He's going to use that artifact for this final step, and we don't know what that step is exactly. But I know that I'm connected to it. I have to stop what he's doing. And I don't want to lose you."

Max kissed her hard, and she felt his wolf brush against hers, those two paranormal parts of them yearning for each other just as much as the human parts did.

"I'm not going to lose you, Cheyenne. If you fall today, I'll fall right with you."

She put her hands over his lips. "Don't say that. Never say that. If I fall, you have to keep fighting. You can't let Blade hurt anyone. You can't let Blade win."

"If you die because you're trying to stop him, then part of me knows he's already won."

"Be selfish right now, say the words, but don't actually go through with it."

"I love you, Cheyenne. I don't think I can fight the way I need to if you fall right now."

"Then do it for me. Avenge me if you have to. But don't die.

"Then you can't die either." He kissed her again, and she closed her eyes, falling more in love with him than she ever thought possible.

Gideon walked by then, and she pulled away, looking at her Alpha.

"Are you ready?" she asked, knowing that he was missing his mate and his daughter fiercely.

"We're getting there. Take some time for yourself, Cheyenne. I know we're relying on you, but it's still a lot to put on your shoulders. Just know you're not alone. We're all here for you. If you can somehow use the Pack bonds to help you do whatever you need to do, pull them through Max, pull them through me. I'm strong enough to handle it. And your mate is strong enough, too."

She nodded, her wolf calming at the sound of her Alpha, who was getting so fierce, so dominant, that it was sometimes hard for her to be in the same room with him. That'd been easier when she was human, but as a wolf, she was still trying to find her place in the hierarchy of dominance.

Gideon had said it would take time, but sometimes, she was afraid that she didn't have much time left. Gideon gave her a nod and then went over to talk with Parker and some of the others.

Most of the Brentwoods were there, ready to fight. Gideon was there, of course, arranging everything with most of the Alphas. Brie and her daughter were back at the den. Brie was not a fighter. She stayed in the den to soothe those who were frightened because they couldn't fight. Not all shifters were fighters. Just like not all humans were.

The Talons didn't even have all of their own fighters on the battlefield that day. Some had to remain behind to protect the den, and protect what was left of their way of life if they were to lose today.

Finn was on the battlefield, along with his mate, Brynn. Those two were very dominant and strong fighters. They needed to be there. Finn and his father represented the Redwoods, along with a lot of the older hierarchy in that Pack. So Finn's uncles were there, but not his cousins. The Redwoods had decided to do that to protect their den because they had such depth in their power.

The Talons didn't have that depth, not in the way the Redwoods did. They had been forced to send a lot of their own leaders, but they also had a lot more dominant wolves like Max who weren't in the hierarchy itself. So those had been left behind to protect the den. The lieutenants like Shane and Bram and Charlotte were also back in the den, safeguarding their own.

While Ryder, the Heir, was there because he wanted to

keep his wife safe. If there were another choice, Cheyenne was pretty sure that Ryder would be back at the den protecting his people. But his wife was a water witch, possibly the strongest one in the history of the world. She was on the battlefield along with the other witches of the den and the Coven to do what they could to protect the world. And Ryder would be there to catch his wife when she fell. Because he seemed certain she would fall.

Apparently, Leah didn't know when to stop. She put her all into everything she did, no matter the cost. Cheyenne didn't know if that would actually be the case this time, considering they had left their child back with the other children in the den. Leah had other things to fight for these days, and something to go home to. That changed things.

Parker was there because he knew the other Packs better than anyone. But his two mates, Brandon and Avery, were at the den.

Brandon, as the Omega, was better suited helping those in the den with their anxiety, rather than those on the battlefield itself.

And Avery, while she was getting better at fighting, had chosen to stay behind to make sure Parker could focus on fighting rather than protecting her.

Mitchell and Kameron were there to fight, but their mates, Dawn and Dhani, had stayed behind, the two of them not yet ready to battle. Although Cheyenne knew that Dhani had rebelled against that idea. She was a witch, and a very strong one, but she would do better protecting the den and keeping the wards up in case Blade came at them from another angle.

Walker was there, but as the Healer, he needed to be. Aimee was back in the den, as well, still not up to fighting shape.

But Cheyenne knew if they lost today, the Talon den would be the first place Blade went. That meant those who got left behind would have to be ready to fight no matter what.

There were so many people Cheyenne didn't know, so many ready to lay their lives down for those they loved and those who were part of their Pack.

Cheyenne knew she wasn't up to fighting strength. She might be a wolf now, might be able to fight Aimee and even Max during training, but she could never win hand-to-hand or fang-to-fang in a real battle.

That wasn't her lot, wasn't her duty today.

Today, she was going to try to stop the artifact.

And if she succeeded, the others could take down Blade.

That was the hope, at least. And that was what she prayed to the moon goddess.

"I think it's time." Her fingers buzzed, and she looked down at them, instinctively knowing that Blade was coming.

"Are you sure? Can you feel him?" Max asked the question quietly, but Gideon and the other Alphas were suddenly surrounding her in the next instant.

Max stiffened, and she knew his wolf was fighting all of the dominant wolves around her, at least mentally. He didn't like when other men were close, at least single men. And, apparently, Allister was single. Max would get over that eventually, all wolves did. But he was newly mated and, sometimes, he let it get the best of him.

Cheyenne put her hand, tingling sensations and all, on his chest and let out a breath.

"My fingers are tingling, and I feel like the artifact is near. I'm not connected to Blade, don't get me wrong, that would be very weird, though not unheard of considering this Pack."

Gideon snorted, and it was the first time that he had sounded at least a little bit relaxed since she had met him.

"I just think he's here."

One of the wolf sentries ran up and whispered something into Kade's ear. The Alpha of the Redwood Pack gave a tight nod before speaking. "She's right. The Aspens just showed up. Not all of them, but some of their most dominant wolves. I don't think there are any cats or anything else that might be hidden within that den. But I have a feeling that there may be more waiting."

"I don't know about that," Audrey said as she made her way over to them.

Audrey was pale and looked like she could use at least a month's worth of food and sleep before she was at full strength, but Cheyenne knew the other woman had to be here today.

"What do you mean?" Gideon asked. He folded his hands over his chest, and Cheyenne knew he wasn't trying to be intimidating, that was just how he stood. The male was intimidating no matter what he did.

"I mean that not all of the Aspens are on his side. But he has some of the strongest wolves out there. And it's not what is going to be out there, it's what will be hidden. He still has witches. Scarlett may be dead, but he still has power. If you can take out his men, then the next of the hierarchy will come in. I'm going to fight as much as I can, but if he orders me to stop, I'll have to fight my own cat, too. Do you understand that?"

Audrey was still part of the Aspen Pack. She hadn't cut her ties. She had explained that she needed to remain Beta despite her Alpha, because she needed to protect those who needed help. There were those in the Aspen Pack who were good but had been cowed and ordered not to do anything. Even the Alpha's son hadn't been seen in ages because Blade had made it so. So, Cheyenne understood that Audrey had her own loyalties, and it wasn't to the Alpha of the Aspen Pack but to those *in* the Aspen Pack who needed her.

"You're going to fight on the other end," Gideon said. "We'll figure out exactly where Blade is, and we'll make sure we hide you. You fighting alongside us...you're a blessing. You've already helped us so much, and if you don't want to fight right now, if you want to stay back and heal and be ready to take care of your Pack when the end comes, you are more than welcome to do that. Because, Audrey? We're going to need you when this is over. So, stay alive, stay safe. And stay out of Blade's sight."

Audrey met Gideon's gaze for a moment before lowering hers. Then she looked over at Cheyenne and held out her hand. Cheyenne frowned and held out hers, as well, grasping the other woman's palm.

"Cheyenne, thank you. I'm sorry I couldn't stop him from attaching you to the artifact. But if you do what I think you're about to do, I hope you find a way to make it through."

Max growled. "What do you know?"

Audrey held up both hands, her eyes wide. "All I know is that Blade is trying to use whatever that artifact is to take out as many people as he can at once and show his power. And if you're saying that she's the Conduit between Blade and the artifact, then maybe she can stop him. But I know as well as you that it's dangerous. That's all I'm saying. You know more than I do. I'm just saying thank you."

Cheyenne put her hand on Max's arm and gave it a squeeze. "It's okay. I knew what she meant. But I think it's time."

The Alphas gave the orders, and soon, everyone was as ready as they were going to be. All of the wolves looked at one another and practically moved in unison before they slowly walked through the forest to the clearing.

Cheyenne's hands shook, but she was ready. She had to be. Those she cared about surrounded her, and the man she loved was right by her side.

She could do this.

They made their way to the clearing. Blade and his men stood across the way. Not a single woman was part of the crew, even the witches were males now. Cheyenne had to wonder what Blade thought about that, or if he had done it on purpose. Considering what she knew about the man, he'd probably done it on purpose because he was a misogynistic prick.

Blade seemed to sense that something had changed when everyone took their positions, and then Cheyenne watched as Gideon nodded at Leah. The woman of the Talon Pack, the strongest witch of their time, lowered her hands, and the wards fell.

Blade growled, and the Aspens moved into position. But nobody attacked.

Cheyenne knew the time for attack would come, but first, Blade had work to do. So she reached out and gripped Max's hand, knowing that she would need him.

Knowing that this was her time.

The moon goddess whispered in her ear, the warmth and strength that filled her seemingly out of nowhere surprising the hell out of her.

Close your eyes. Believe in yourself. Close the Conduit. Wrap

yourself around the power and close it. You can do this, Cheyenne.
I believe in you.

And then, the moon goddess moved through her, warming her from the inside. Cheyenne threw her head back and screamed as Blade gripped the artifact in his hand. People were looking all around, wondering what was happening, but Cheyenne knew.

This was a battle between her and Blade, with the moon goddess all around.

Cheyenne was the Conduit, the one in between.

But she couldn't do this by herself. She couldn't stop the immense power slamming into her from either side without the bond she knew had been made for this purpose—and for so much more.

In her head, Cheyenne heard Max scream, and she squeezed his hand, the bond between them flaring.

People fell to their knees all around them, and she knew that the artifact was slowly leaching their power from them, then moving it through her to the Aspen Alpha. Blade shouted from the other side of the clearing, and Cheyenne knew that she wasn't stopping the power, he was still stealing it and taking it into himself.

This had to stop. Max whispered into her ear, only she thought maybe it was just in her head. She didn't know anymore.

"Take what you can from me. We can do this together. It's not just you who's the Conduit, I'm here, too. Use our bond. Use me. I love you."

And she loved him. But she couldn't say anything, could only open her mouth in a silent scream. But she did as the moon goddess had told her to do, she wrapped her power around the cord that connected her to the artifact and the one that tethered her to Max.

Heat blazed, and she shook, falling to her knees. She knew that Max was holding her, but he was falling, as well. People were shouting all around them, and light blazed, but she couldn't focus on that.

She could only concentrate on closing down the power, severing the loop. And with her power mixed in with Max's, she knew she could do it.

So she tugged on the power that connected her to Max and pushed it towards the artifact itself.

Blade screamed, and she opened her eyes to watch the Aspen Alpha fall to his knees. Blood filled his mouth and rolled down his chin, but he was healing right before their eyes.

But the artifact wasn't.

In fact, the stone had a huge crack in it, and as Blade clenched his fist, it's slowly turned to dust, the winds taking it as the moon goddess let out a soft sigh in Cheyenne's mind.

She knew the moon goddess was hurt, but she didn't know what that meant.

But as Cheyenne got to her feet, still holding Max's hand, all of the other wolves on her side of the battle looked at them. Their eyes wide, one by one, they went to their knees. The Alphas went to their knees.

And she had no idea why.

"That is what Blade was missing," Gideon said, his voice reverent.

And then the moon goddess spoke to all of them, her voice filling the field, though she wasn't corporeal.

Here are your Supreme Alphas. There was never one. It was always a pair. They are the ones who will take these wolves, these cats, and all of my other creations into the new world. They are the ones you will answer to. Not this man who defiles our greatest lore. They are the Supreme Alphas. And they are mine.

She screamed the last word, her pain so deep that tears filled Cheyenne's eyes.

Cheyenne looked up at her mate, her fellow Supreme Alpha, and knew the world had changed yet again.

CHAPTER SEVENTEEN

Max nearly fell to his knees again, wondering what had just happened. Power thrummed through his veins, power that had been there all along, waiting, anticipating.

And now it was free because of a goddess he had never met but heard and loved and worshiped.

One who had given him his mate.

His future.

But there wasn't time to think, wasn't time to wonder what would happen now that the moon goddess had declared him and his mate the Supreme Alphas.

He would think about the details of that later, wonder about the ramifications of what had just occurred.

Now, it was time to fight.

Because Blade was ready to go. The blood had been wiped from his chin, the artifact long gone. But the man was still a wolf, still an Alpha with immense strength, and he still had magic surrounding him thanks to his witches.

It was time for the battle to truly begin.

Cheyenne pulled Max against her and kissed him. "I'm going to fight by your side," she said. "And you can't stop me."

"I'd rather have you by my side than anywhere else. Because you're mine, Alpha."

Her eyes widened, and she shook her head. There would be time to talk later. To understand. "Okay, then, let's fight."

Max kissed her hard, and then they were off.

Kameron fought alongside them, his claws out as he took down one of the wolves coming at them. Some of the Aspens were in human form, others in wolf form. It was the same with their own Packs, but it was insane how many Aspens there were. Audrey had said that not all of the Aspens were there, that, in fact, most of them were not. And yet the number of men that Blade had with him that called themselves Aspens, or were at least allied with them, was far more than all of the men and women they had, combined with the humans, the Coven, the Redwoods, the Thames, and the Centrals.

No wonder they hadn't been able to defeat the Aspens until now—because Max knew they would win today. They had to. It had taken combining the true power of so many on one side, despite any of their differences, to make it here.

And Max wasn't going to lose today.

So he took out one wolf, his claws bared. Cheyenne did the same with her blade, but she was lower to the ground, using the fighting stances she had learned in training. She was slower, not as good as the rest of them, but she had far less training, too.

She was still doing fantastically. And any wolf that got too close to her, he gutted with his bare hands.

One of the Aspen wolves jumped at Max's face, and he clawed the asshole's eyes out. It fell to the ground with a whimper, and he killed it quickly, snapping its neck. He didn't want any of them to feel too much pain, only Blade deserved that.

Max knew what it felt like to almost die on a field just like this, and he knew the horror that dawned when you were too hurt to do anything but hope someone might save your life. Or put you out of your misery.

He didn't wish that on anyone, except for maybe Blade.

And maybe if Max were a better person, he wouldn't have wished it on anyone at all, but he wasn't a better person. All he wanted was revenge against Blade. The man had almost killed his mate, multiple times. Had nearly killed those close to his family.

And Blade deserved what was coming to him.

But the others, those who followed blindly...maybe they didn't deserve that horror. So Max would make it quick. Would make it easy.

That would be their mercy.

Not their lives.

If they fought against those who just wanted peace? Then they didn't deserve a second chance. Or a third. Or a fourth.

Max pulled Cheyenne out of the way as one of the wolves came at her, and she wasn't able to duck in time. It hit Max in the shoulder, its fangs sliding through his skin. He growled and then punched the shit out of it. Cheyenne didn't have her claws out, wasn't able to yet, but she did have a knife. She was a vet, after all, and she was decent with a blade, even though she never liked when he joked about that.

Max grunted at the pain of the bite but ignored it. But then, Walker was right there, his hands on Max's shoulder for one second. And then the pain was gone.

His Healer cousin ran off, actually running towards where Mitchell was now, to put his hands on Max's brother. Mitchell had a huge laceration on his gut, one that would've been fatal for any human, but thank the goddess they were all wolves. Parker held Mitchell up, making sure no one came at any of them as the wolves continued their attack. There were fire witches, water witches, all types of magic users throwing power at them. But Leah and the other Coven members were ready. Max watched as they used their combined powers to create a force field of water, fire, and earth. They threw back whatever the Aspen witches sent towards them.

And though Leah was the strongest, and the Coven was pretty damn strong, they didn't use dark magic. And so, the Aspen witches were equal in power because they used dark magic. Because they sacrificed their blood and the blood and lives of the other Aspen Pack members at their disposal.

They literally used the deaths of their own to create stronger magic, and that made Max want to throw up. But he ignored that and went back to fighting the wolves in front of him.

Mitchell was up on his feet again, only wavering a little bit and shaking his head. Walker growled, but then he had to go because one of the other Talon wolves was hurt.

Out of all of them, Walker would probably end up the most drained by the end if they weren't careful. His cousin put everything he could into saving his people, and if he didn't watch it, he'd put too much.

And Walker didn't have his mate with him to protect him this time. To make sure he didn't cross that line. But others were there to make sure he didn't. Parker let Mitchell go off with one of the other Redwood wolves and followed Walker, most likely screaming at him to take care of himself.

All of them took care of each other, and Max was no different. He threw a wolf off one of the Redwood members, one named Maddox, the former Omega of the Pack before he'd given up the title to the next generation.

Max knew him well and refused to let Maddox die today because of someone else's rage.

Then, Max when to Cheyenne's side again, and the two of them fought off two more wolves and a witch who tried to get at them. And yet, it was Gideon, Kade, Cole, and Allister who fought Blade now. No one could get to the group of Alphas that were fighting each other, yet they still tried to help.

But because Blade had four witches using death magic surrounding him, there was no way for anyone to get near unless something changed.

Max growled and ran past Finn and Brynn, who were fighting another set of wolves and witches. Cheyenne was right by his side, staying out of most of the horror, and he was grateful for that. Her job was done, and theoretically, she should've left, but for some reason, the moon goddess had made them both Supreme Alphas—and that meant they were going to fight together.

They weren't going to let anyone fall.

They wouldn't leave anyone behind.

And, somehow, Max and Cheyenne would make sure that the witches using death magic died.

Because, if they were gone, the other Alphas—or even he and Cheyenne, new Alphas in however the moon goddess intended—could maybe take out Blade.

"I can help you with the witches," Audrey said, coming up from behind them, blood covering her but not her own from the scent of it. Good.

Max looked over at the lion shifter. "Are you sure? How?"

"As soon as he sees me, he'll want to come after me, and that means the witches will focus their magic on me, as well. Use me as bait and get in there and kill those witches. They should be exhausted by now because Blade doesn't know how to protect them. So, make sure they see me, make sure it looks like I'm weak, and then get in there and take them out. The other Alphas can get Blade. You just have to make sure you get those witches."

"Okay, but don't you dare die. I'm going to hate if you die." Cheyenne was the one to say this, and Max nodded. "Got me?"

"She's right," Max added. "You might not be a Talon, but you're an honorary one. And we don't take kindly to our people dying."

Audrey gave a ghost of a smile before nodding. "I don't plan on dying. My Pack needs me. Now, let's go."

Then, the three of them were off, doing their best to try and get into Blade's line of sight. Finally, Audrey screamed. She screamed like the weight of a thousand terrors were on her shoulders and years of pain and exile had been pulled out of her.

Max moved out of the way, knowing that she needed to be the bait, yet knowing they wouldn't let her die either.

Blade finally looked over, his eyes wide. Max had never

seen so much anger, horror, and hatred in a man's eyes before.

Blade hated Audrey with every ounce of his being.

And Blade would die today.

There wasn't another option.

Suddenly, Blade moved forward, the witches turning to look at Audrey, as well. And, in that instant, Max knew that what Audrey had said was the exact opposite of what needed to happen. Audrey would be safe if she stayed behind and, thankfully, she did. Max and Cheyenne moved up as one, and each of the Alphas of the Packs took out a witch.

Gideon took care of air.

Kade defeated fire.

Cole handled earth.

And Allister slew water.

The four witches who had used their power for death and destruction crumpled in front of the Alphas as each of them took out one who dared to harm their Packs, who helped to take out the wards of each of their dens over time.

These four witches with no names had been part of Scarlett's crew.

They'd been part of what Blade needed to kill so many of them time and time again.

And, as the other wolves from the Aspen Pack fought all of the other Packs, humans, and the Coven, Blade was by himself, standing amongst the ruins of his power, the remnants of his greed.

And then the Alpha who had declared himself more didn't have time to tell his story, to give a diatribe about what he had done and why he had done it.

He'd had enough time to talk. Had more than enough opportunity to tell them of his greed.

They didn't need to hear any more.

Blade didn't have to say anything.

Instead, Max and Cheyenne ran as one, and Max jumped on Blade, throwing him onto the grass. In an instant, Max was transported back to a time when he was the one on the ground, his arm splayed out, his other arm having been half blown off in an explosion. He remembered looking up into the eyes of a human as the other man practically vivisected him on the field. And, all at once, Max knew he couldn't wait any longer to end Blade. Blade might deserve horror and pain, but Max wouldn't be the one to give it to him.

It was true then, apparently, that he wouldn't wish that on anyone.

Not even his greatest enemy.

Cheyenne stood above him, ready to fight, prepared to attack.

And Max looked up at his mate, knowing that he wasn't alone.

He would never be alone again.

And then he broke Blade's neck. One crack. The end.

There wasn't any pain. Wasn't any terror.

Max had lived through enough pain and horror for a lifetime. And he wasn't going to wait for Blade to find a way out of it.

The man had seen his empire fall, had seen those he used and abused attack him.

He had seen the artifact he had put his entire life into finding and using fade away to dust.

And he saw the goddess that he'd apparently thought to make use of reject him and give the power he coveted to those he had tried to kill.

That was the torture the man received.

And, wherever Blade was now, maybe he found the torture he truly deserved.

Or maybe he found the peace he never had.

Because now, Max knew that he and his people would finally be able to find their own peace.

Because the evil Alpha was dead.

The terror was gone.

Those who fought with Blade screamed in horror, the Pack bonds of hierarchy changing as the Alpha was now dead, and there would be a new Alpha, Heir, and so many other positions filled as those who died vacated the roles.

The Aspens fell, but not the Pack itself. Audrey stood in the remnants of the battle, and Max knew there would be more to come. There would be more they needed to talk about, so much more. But Blade lay dead beneath him, and the other Alphas came to make sure, to ask questions, but Max didn't hear any of it.

Instead, he turned to his mate and pulled her to his chest.

The battle was over. Peace had yet to come. But part of it was over, at least.

Maybe now he could sleep.

Maybe now he could rest.

Maybe now he could believe.

CHAPTER EIGHTEEN

They say at the end of a battle, that some can see the heavens, that others can only breathe in their hells.

Cheyenne had never known exactly what that meant until these recent weeks. In the days since the battle, in the weeks since Blade was no more, the idea of restructuring and settling into peace hadn't settled easily on everybody's shoulders.

But to Cheyenne, it was almost as if it were a new birth.

She wasn't the Cheyenne she had been before. But then again, she wasn't the Cheyenne she'd thought to become either.

She was the Cheyenne she needed to be, the Cheyenne that Max wanted her to be.

Her mate, her co-Supreme Alpha.

What a strange world it was, what a strangely odd and yet thrilling world.

She sat in her room that she shared with Max, in the house that he had built for himself but that they now were making their own.

She was no longer in *his* home, but theirs. And she was within her den, with her Pack, but she also had a new title that they were only just starting to learn about.

Gideon was the Talon Pack Alpha until he decided to step down, and his daughter, Fallon, took his place. Of course, first, she would become Heir once Ryder was ready to step down. But that would be many, many years from now. Maybe even a century or more.

Because there was peace. Finally, there would be peace for the Talons.

Cheyenne could feel it in every breath she took, in every day that passed as their wards grew strong, and their people finally came out into the daylight as if they could breathe again.

Only this time, there was one that could connect them all—*two* that could connect them all.

The moon goddess had declared Cheyenne and Max the Supreme Alphas.

And that was such a strange title to her, that she had only taken it as a joke at first. She'd thought, surely, it had to be a joke when it came to Blade. But now, it was truth.

They needed to decide what would happen, and where

they would live, and how the idea of having one large Pack would work. But for now, she would live within the Talon den with her mate.

The others around the field had heard what happened, and because it was the moon goddess herself that had made the proclamation, her voice loud, strained, in pain yet powerful, people had taken to calling her and Max "Alpha."

To say that her life had completely changed would be an understatement.

In the coming years, they would decide what it meant to be the Supreme Alphas, but Parker had begun to pave the road already.

When he became the Voice of the Wolves, a title that hadn't been used in centuries but one the moon goddess herself had given to him, he had connected the Packs. Even if it was just the idea of a treaty or a way to message or contact one another. The Packs in this country and around the world had a small thread of connection.

And now Parker would be the one to help them realize exactly what it meant to be the one the Alphas answered to.

For now, Cheyenne knew the Alphas wouldn't be forced to answer to her and Max in a way that negated the Alphas' powers, but they could be the ones that made sure whatever happened with Blade didn't happen again. And ensure that no wolves succumbed to summoning a demon from the underworld. Or even allowing the Pack to disintegrate within itself.

Someone needed to make sure the Packs were healthy, that they were being heard.

Being cut off from each other and the rest of the world for centuries had been important and needed, but it had hurt some in the end. So, Max and Cheyenne would find a way to make sure all of the Packs were heard and would be cared for. And maybe, if needed, they would be relegated. She didn't want to be that kind of Alpha, she wasn't even sure she liked the title at all, but the moon goddess had given it to her, and she was going to learn what it meant.

But she had her mate by her side, her love, and she knew they could make it through.

"You're thinking about the title again, aren't you?" Max asked as he came forward. He kissed her softly, and she sighed. She loved this man with all of her heart. He had surprised her at every turn, with every breath. She still couldn't believe that he was hers.

She couldn't believe that she was actually going to be around to see those end of days. She'd thought she would die at that battle, and she knew Max had thought so, too.

But they'd both won. And had found a new purpose.

They'd been fighting for each other that day.

And now they had time.

Time.

Time to figure out what this new world meant for them and how they would create a family together.

Because they wanted pups, they wanted a future, they wanted a life. And now they had a chance for it all.

She finally leaned back and spoke. "I just don't know if we're going to be allowed to stay here? I mean, are we?"

Max nodded. "We'll always have a home here, and we'll always be Talon Pack members, even if the bonds are slightly different."

Her bonds to the Talon Pack had changed since the moon goddess spoke. Cheyenne could still feel them, but it was as if the connection meant that they were loved by the Talon Pack but not fully a part of them. And then, a week after the battle, she and Max had each woken up in the middle of the night, clutching at their hearts, a thread of power now connected to the Redwood Pack surprising them. And then a week later, the Central Pack. A week after that, the Thames Pack.

It seemed that they would be connected to every single Pack that they made a personal connection with over time.

That was what it meant to be the Supreme Alphas. Her bonds weren't like those that Gideon had with his Pack, and she realized that after she had asked him straight out what would happen to her and Max.

Nobody knew exactly, but they knew that they would figure it out together.

So far, the world hadn't turned against them, but that didn't mean it wouldn't happen eventually.

"So we don't have to leave?" She bit her lip. "At least not yet?"

He shook his head and then kissed her again. "No, we don't have to leave. But we may one day find a home outside the den, much like some of the wolves did in the past. Not everybody has always lived within the den. It was only recently that we were forced to because of the war with the humans and then with Blade. But if we're not at war, then we can live anywhere we want. And you know Kade said that we could have a home in the Redwood den if we wanted to. And we could. We could go hang out with my cousin and see her babies grow and maybe watch our babies grow up there. If we ever want to visit Europe and see the lands there, Allister said we can come visit the Thames Pack. And you know Audrey said that the Aspens are open to us, as well."

She nodded. The connection to the Aspen Pack had shown up after the one with the Thames. It was fragile at best, tattered and frayed at worst. Blade's son had been chosen by the moon goddess as the new Alpha, and every other member of their hierarchy that had been corrupted by evil had either died on that battlefield or turned to dust right after Blade died.

Cheyenne knew that was due to the moon goddess. And she wondered what the goddess had sacrificed to make it happen.

Because there was a reason the goddess hadn't stepped in before this, hadn't sacrificed more than she had.

Goddesses and gods weren't supposed to play with humanity and shifters, but she had...more than once.

And Cheyenne wondered what would happen next.

"Chase is the Alpha? Right?" she asked, her voice soft.

"Yes, and Audrey is helping him as Beta. Chase was gone for a while, he hadn't been able to come back thanks to his dad. But there's a new Alpha, a new hierarchy, and the Aspen Pack is going to get healthy eventually. And I think maybe we'll be able to help that. I don't know how exactly, but the goddess gave us this power, this role, for a reason."

"I don't want to take advantage of it or forget about it. I want to help. When I first realized I was going to be a Talon Pack member, I tried my best to think about exactly where I was going to fit in and how I could help out. That's why I threw myself into being the Conduit."

Max nodded. "I understand, believe me, I understand. I threw myself into being a council member and then helping you figure out exactly how we were going to stop Blade. I never truly felt like I belonged. And then, I did. I did because of you. And now we have a role, a title, and a place. And we're going to make sure that the shifters of this world understand that they are not forgotten, they are not left behind because they are different."

"We're going to take care of our people, Max. We're going to find a way to protect them all."

And then her mate kissed her, and she fell in love with him all over again.

She was a Pack member, but she was more than that. She was a shifter. She was an Alpha. And she was mate to one of the greatest men she'd ever known.

And this was just the beginning for her.

For them.

EPILOGUE

Max sat in Gideon's house, and this time he didn't feel like he was on the outside looking in. This was his home, his family. And even though he and Cheyenne would soon be leaving the den to go and visit the other Packs around the United States and then the world, these were the people in his life that he would always have in his heart. There would be centuries with these people, and he'd already had over a century with most of them. He couldn't wait to see where they ended up next. But this was his family, his heart.

No matter where he went, they would always be with him.

Much like the woman at his side.

Cheyenne smiled up at him before moving back to talk with Dhani about something important.

They were leaving the next morning to visit the Aspens before they headed over to the other side of the country. The President of the United States wanted to meet with them so they would get that out of the way before they went to meet with the other Packs. The President was on the shifters' side and actually had a family member who was part of a Pack, so it wouldn't be dangerous. It would just be another momentous occasion in a very long year of change for them.

"I can't believe that you're leaving us, at least for a little bit," Gideon said. Max met his Alpha's eyes and realized, once again, that he *could* meet his cousin's gaze and not back down. Because Max was an Alpha now, too. He would always think of Gideon as his Alpha, his family. But, technically, Gideon wasn't his Alpha anymore. That didn't change the way he felt, though. He was inside Gideon's den, Gideon's territory, so Gideon was Alpha here. Max didn't know how exactly things would work when they visited the other dens, but that was something he and Cheyenne would figure out together. They actually planned to bring a few wolves from the Talons and the Redwoods with them, wolves that wanted to take the journey and roam. They weren't ready to leave their Packs but wanted to see the world. So, they would be part of his and Cheyenne's detail. They wouldn't be Packmates, wouldn't be his Pack or hers, but they would be there so he and Cheyenne weren't completely alone when they visited the world.

He and Cheyenne figure that's how things would work out eventually, them picking up random wolves and even cats along the way. Perhaps even some other shifter types if they discovered them. They would find who worked well with them for a little bit, and maybe even sometimes a bit longer, and their detail would have a never-ending supply of people who wanted to see the world.

It was a different way for a wolf, but after so many years of trying to find their way, he felt like this would work for them. He could feel it in his bones.

"I'm not leaving for long," Max said.

"I know, but it still feels like you were just a little baby boy running around with your little cloth diaper."

"Thank you for that image. Make sure you tell Cheyenne that before we leave."

Gideon threw back his head and laughed. "Oh, don't worry, I already did." Fallon ran up to them at that moment, and Gideon leaned down to pick up his baby girl. She wasn't a baby anymore, but she was still young enough to be Gideon's little girl. Of course, when Fallon ended up being the Alpha of the Talon Pack in many, *many* years, Gideon would probably still think of her as his little girl. Woe be to anyone who dared come into Fallon's life and want to be her mate.

Brie waddled out of the kitchen and towards them, heavily pregnant with the couple's second child.

Max just grinned as Gideon's eyes glowed gold with

such possessiveness that Max wasn't sure that Brie wouldn't just melt on the spot.

Brie was going to drop that baby at any moment, and it was insane that Gideon was actually calm enough to allow her around so many other people. It probably helped that they were family.

Max talked with his cousin for a little bit longer before turning to Brynn and Finn, who were watching Mackenzie dance around them, Brynn heavily pregnant with twins. Apparently, once a battle with a dangerous egomaniac Alpha ended, everybody went and got pregnant. He and Cheyenne were waiting a little bit longer before they started a family because they needed to figure out exactly what this Supreme Alpha business meant. But they would have a family, a large one if he and Cheyenne had anything to say about it.

"I can't wait for you to come and hang out with our Pack," Brynn said with a smile. "I mean, it's not like you've ever spent any time at the Redwoods'." Finn rolled his eyes and kissed his mate's head, his hand possessively landing on her stomach. Max just laughed and talked with his cousin for a bit longer before moving on to the next couple.

Ryder and Leah were feeding each other from opposite plates like they were hopelessly-in-love newlyweds instead of having been mated for a few years already. The two were disgustingly sweet with one another, and their son,

Bryson, was off chasing Fallon, who, in turn, chased him back. It reminded Max of how he and Brynn had used to play years ago. Ryder and Leah hadn't started on a second child yet, but they had been thinking about it. Max figured by the time he saw his cousin again, the couple would have another child, maybe even two. Because the way Leah kept watching the pregnant women walk around the room, he could see the yearning in her eyes.

Cheyenne had moved over to speak with Charlotte, Bram, and Shane. The three were holding their newborn twins, each rotating the two babies as they spoke. Genetically, the children were clearly Bram's with their dark skin, but Shane was also their father in every way that mattered. Max figured that the next babies Charlotte had would be genetically Shane's, and no matter what, they would be considered full siblings. Because that's exactly how triads worked within the Packs, and Max was thankful for it.

Speaking of triads, Parker, Brandon, and Avery were sprawled out on one of the couches in a heated discussion about birth canals. Max really didn't want to know *why* they were talking about that, but the three were talking loudly enough that pretty much the whole room could hear. Avery lay against Parker with her feet up in Brandon's lap, her ankles so swollen that Max was worried she would never be able to walk again. She was having a difficult pregnancy but wasn't letting anything stop her from doing what she needed to do. Since she was going to drop a set of triplets any day now, she was likely beyond ready for labor. It was insane that so many twins and triplets were being born into his family, but after having so many years without having any children born into the Pack at all, apparently, the Brentwoods were making up for lost time.

Mitchell held his baby son in his arms as Dawn worked on making the bottle for him. She'd also had a difficult pregnancy and had needed to go straight to formula instead of breastfeeding thanks to it. He didn't ask questions but knew that Dawn had talked to Cheyenne about it a lot. But any time that Dawn needed extra help with the baby in the middle of the night, Max and Cheyenne were right there. This was his nephew, not a second cousin. And though he felt all the newborns and children were all his nephews and nieces, this baby was special. Because he was the first one born to Mitchell and Max's branch of the family.

He couldn't help but be a little selfish with the baby's time.

Walker and Kameron were in a heated discussion about sports for some unknown reason. Max vaguely remembered them talking about sports before, and he figured that it was something the two decided they needed to talk about so they didn't have to talk about their daily duties. Max didn't mind, but he really had no idea what they were talking about.

Aimee and Dhani had now moved in on Cheyenne,

tears running down their faces as Dawn walked over, leaving the baby with Mitchell so the four women could hug each other. Aimee and Dhani were both pregnant, as well, though not as far along as the rest of them. Max figured he and Cheyenne would be back soon for those babies' births.

So many babies, so little time.

It was going to take him forever to learn all their names, but he didn't mind. He had a whole world to see, a new set of Packs that needed his and Cheyenne's guidance and presence.

He would never encroach on another Alpha, not unless there was a dire need to, but he knew that everything happened for a reason, even if he hated that phrase with all his might.

"I'd like to make a toast," Gideon said, pulling Max out of his thoughts.

All of the couples went back to one another, Cheyenne moving up to his side. He held her close, kissing the top of her head. She put her fingers in his belt loops, and he smiled. He loved when she did that.

"To Max and Cheyenne. Our Supreme Alphas, our protectors, and our family. Know that you are always welcome here, that you are always Talon Pack. No matter where you go, no matter the people you meet, know that you are ours, and you are loved. Thank you for saving us, thank you for being strong enough to do what was meant to be done. And thank you for being true to yourselves.

May the goddess bless you more than she already has, and may your futures be bright, and whole."

Everyone raised his or her glass, and Max wiped the tears from Cheyenne's face after they each took a drink.

"Thank you, Gideon. For everything." Max's voice was low but sure. Proud.

He kissed his mate as the others kissed their mates, as well. And Max looked down at the woman by his side, knowing he had been whole long before the battle ended.

Cheyenne was his bonded mate, was his thread back to himself thanks to the moon goddess. But it was the woman herself who had brought him out of his shell and made him the man he needed to be.

"I love you, Cheyenne Brentwood. With everything in my heart."

"I think I love you more, Max."

"You think?"

"Well, I guess you're just going to have to keep showing me how much you love me so I can make sure that I'm right on schedule."

Max rolled his eyes and then kissed her again.

And as he and Cheyenne left the den the next day, the wolves and witches and cat from the Talons howled and screeched and shouted to the goddess. It was a fine goodbye for a wolf who thought he had no place. For a man who had thought he lost everything and found more than he'd ever dreamt of.

The Talons were home, they were family, they were Pack.

And Max and Cheyenne would never be forgotten.

THE END

The Talon Pack series might be over, but there will be more shifters to come.

Soon.

A NOTE FROM CARRIE ANN

Thank you so much for reading FOREVER BROKEN! I do hope if you liked this story, that you would please leave a review! Reviews help authors and readers.

The Talon Pack series is complete but I'm not done yet!

Is that the last of the world that holds the Redwood Pack and the Talon Pack?

I sure hope not.

Just wait and see...

If you want to make sure you know what's coming next from me, you can sign up for my newsletter at www.CarrieAnnRyan.com; follow me on twitter at @CarrieAnnRyan, or like my Facebook page. I also have a Facebook Fan Club where we have trivia, chats, and other goodies. You guys are the reason I get to do what I do and I thank you.

Make sure you're signed up for my MAILING LIST so you can know when the next releases are available as well as find giveaways and FREE READS.

Happy Reading!

The Talon Pack:

    Book 1: <u>Tattered Loyalties</u>

    Book 2: <u>An Alpha's Choice</u>

    Book 3: <u>Mated in Mist</u>

    Book 4: <u>Wolf Betrayed</u>

    Book 5: <u>Fractured Silence</u>

    Book 6: <u>Destiny Disgraced</u>

    Book 7: <u>Eternal Mourning</u>

    Book 8: <u>Strength Enduring</u>

    Book 9: <u>Forever Broken</u>

ABOUT CARRIE ANN RYAN

Carrie Ann Ryan is the New York Times and USA Today bestselling author of contemporary and paranormal romance. Her works include the Montgomery Ink, Redwood Pack, Talon Pack, and Gallagher Brothers series, which have sold over 2.0 million books worldwide. She started writing while in graduate school for her advanced degree in chemistry and hasn't stopped since. Carrie Ann has written over fifty novels and novellas with more in the works. When she's not writing about bearded tattooed men or alpha wolves that need to find their mates, she's reading as much as she can and exploring the world of baking and gourmet cooking.

www.CarrieAnnRyan.com

MORE FROM CARRIE ANN RYAN

The Less Than Series:
A Montgomery Ink Spin Off Series
Book 1: Breathless With Her

Book 2: Reckless With You

The Elements of Five Series:
A YA Fantasty Series
Book 1: From Breath and Ruin

Montgomery Ink:
Book 0.5: Ink Inspired

Book 0.6: Ink Reunited

Book 1: Delicate Ink

Book 1.5: Forever Ink

Book 2: Tempting Boundaries

Book 3: Harder than Words

Book 4: Written in Ink

Book 4.5: Hidden Ink

Book 5: Ink Enduring

Book 6: Ink Exposed

Book 6.5: Adoring Ink

Book 6.6: Love, Honor, & Ink

Book 7: Inked Expressions

Book 7.3: Dropout

Book 7.5: Executive Ink

Book 8: Inked Memories

Book 8.5: Inked Nights

Book 8.7: Second Chance Ink

The Gallagher Brothers Series:
A Montgomery Ink Spin Off Series
Book 1: Love Restored
Book 2: Passion Restored
Book 3: Hope Restored

The Whiskey and Lies Series:
A Montgomery Ink Spin Off Series
Book 1: Whiskey Secrets
Book 2: Whiskey Reveals
Book 3: Whiskey Undone

The Talon Pack:
Book 1: Tattered Loyalties
Book 2: An Alpha's Choice
Book 3: Mated in Mist
Book 4: Wolf Betrayed
Book 5: Fractured Silence
Book 6: Destiny Disgraced
Book 7: Eternal Mourning
Book 8: Strength Enduring
Book 9: Forever Broken

Redwood Pack Series:
Book 1: An Alpha's Path
Book 2: A Taste for a Mate
Book 3: Trinity Bound

Redwood Pack Box Set (Contains Books 1-3)

Book 3.5: A Night Away

Book 4: Enforcer's Redemption

Book 4.5: Blurred Expectations

Book 4.7: Forgiveness

Book 5: Shattered Emotions

Book 6: Hidden Destiny

Book 6.5: A Beta's Haven

Book 7: Fighting Fate

Book 7.5: Loving the Omega

Book 7.7: The Hunted Heart

Book 8: Wicked Wolf

The Complete Redwood Pack Box Set (Contains Books 1-7.7)

The Branded Pack Series:
(Written with Alexandra Ivy)

Book 1: Stolen and Forgiven

Book 2: Abandoned and Unseen

Book 3: Buried and Shadowed

Dante's Circle Series:

Book 1: Dust of My Wings

Book 2: Her Warriors' Three Wishes

Book 3: An Unlucky Moon

The Dante's Circle Box Set (Contains Books 1-3)

Book 3.5: His Choice

Book 4: Tangled Innocence

Book 5: Fierce Enchantment

Book 6: An Immortal's Song

Book 7: Prowled Darkness

The Complete Dante's Circle Series (Contains Books 1-7)

Holiday, Montana Series:

Book 1: Charmed Spirits

Book 2: Santa's Executive

Book 3: Finding Abigail

The Holiday, Montana Box Set (Contains Books 1-3)

Book 4: Her Lucky Love

Book 5: Dreams of Ivory

The Complete Holiday, Montana Box Set (Contains Books 1-5)

The Happy Ever After Series:

Flame and Ink

Ink Ever After

Single Title:

Finally Found You

EXCERPT: WHISKEY SECRETS

From New York Times Bestselling Author Carrie Ann Ryan's Whiskey and Lies

<u>Whiskey Secrets</u>

Shocking pain slammed into his skull and down his back. Dare Collins did his best not to scream in the middle of his own bar. He slowly stood up and rubbed the back of his head since he'd been distracted and hit it on the countertop. Since the thing was made of solid wood and thick as hell, he was surprised he hadn't given himself a concussion. But since he didn't see double, he had a feeling once his long night was over, he'd just have to make the throbbing go away with a glass of Macallan.

There was nothing better than a glass of smooth

whiskey or an ice-cold mug of beer after a particularly long day. Which one Dare chose each night depended on not only his mood but also those around him. So was the life of a former cop turned bartender.

He had a feeling he'd be going for the whiskey and not a woman tonight—like most nights if he were honest. It had been a long day of inventory and no-show staff members. Meaning he had a headache from hell, and it looked as if he'd be working open to close when he truly didn't want to. But that's what happened when one was the owner of a bar and restaurant rather than just a manager or bartender—like he was with the Old Whiskey Restaurant and Bar.

It didn't help that his family had been in and out of the place all day for one reason or another—his brothers and parents either wanting something to eat or having a question that needed to be answered right away where a phone call or text wouldn't suffice. His mom and dad had mentioned more than once that he needed to be ready for their morning meeting, and he had a bad feeling in his gut about what that would mean for him later. But he pushed that from his thoughts because he was used to things in his life changing on a dime. He'd left the force for a reason, after all.

Enough of that.

He loved his family, he really did, but sometimes, they —his parents in particular—gave him a headache.

Since his mom and dad still ran the Old Whiskey Inn

above his bar, they were constantly around, working their tails off at odd jobs that were far too hard for them at their ages, but they were all just trying to earn a living. When they weren't handling business for the inn, they were fixing problems upstairs that Dare wished they'd let him help with.

While he'd have preferred to call it a night and head back to his place a few blocks away, he knew that wouldn't happen tonight. Since his bartender, Rick, had called in sick at the last minute—as well as two of Dare's waitresses from the bar—Dare was pretty much screwed.

And if he wallowed just a little bit more, he might hear a tiny violin playing in his ear. He needed to get a grip and get over it. Working late and dealing with other people's mistakes was part of his job description, and he was usually fine with that.

Apparently, he was just a little off tonight. And since he knew himself well, he had a feeling it was because he was nearing the end of his time without his kid. Whenever he spent too many days away from Nathan, he acted like a crabby asshole. Thankfully, his weekend was coming up.

"Solving a hard math problem over there, or just daydreaming? Because that expression on your face looks like you're working your brain too hard. I'm surprised I don't see smoke coming out of your ears." Fox asked as he walked up to the bar, bringing Dare out of his thoughts. Dare had been pulling drafts and cleaning glasses mindlessly while in his head, but he was glad for the distraction, even if it annoyed him that he needed one.

Dare shook his head and flipped off his brother. "Suck me."

The bar was busy that night, so Fox sat down on one of the empty stools and grinned. "Nice way to greet your customers." He glanced over his shoulder before looking back at Dare and frowning. "Where are Rick and the rest of your staff?"

Dare barely held back a growl. "Out sick. Either there's really a twenty-four-hour stomach bug going around and I'm going to be screwed for the next couple of days, or they're all out on benders."

Fox cursed under his breath before hopping off his stool and going around the side of the large oak and maple bar to help out. That was Dare's family in a nutshell—they dropped everything whenever one of them needed help, and nobody even had to ask for it. Since Dare sucked at asking for help on a good day, he was glad that Fox knew what he needed without him having to say it.

Without asking, Fox pulled up a few drink orders and began mixing them with the skill of a long-time barkeep. Since Fox owned the small town newspaper—the Whiskey Chronicle—Dare was still surprised sometimes at how deft his younger brother was at working alongside him. Of course, even his parents, his older brother Loch, and his younger sister Tabby knew their way around the bar.

Just not as well as Dare did. Considering that this was *his* job, he was grateful for that.

He loved his family, his bar, and hell, he even loved his little town on the outskirts of Philly. Whiskey, Pennsylvania was like most other small towns in his state where some parts were new additions, and others were old stone buildings from the Revolutionary or Civil war eras with add-ons—like his.

And with a place called Whiskey, everyone attached the label where they could. Hence the town paper, his bar, and most of the other businesses around town. Only Loch's business really stood out with Loch's Security and Gym down the street, but that was just like Loch to be a little different yet still part of the town.

Whiskey had been named as such because of its old bootlegging days. It used to be called something else, but since Prohibition, the town had changed its name and cashed in on it. Whiskey was one of the last places in the country to keep Prohibition on the books, even with the nationwide decree. They'd fought to keep booze illegal, not for puritan reasons, but because their bootlegging market had helped the township thrive. Dare knew there was a lot more to it than that, but those were the stories the leaders told the tourists, and it helped with the flare.

Whiskey was located right on the Delaware River, so it overlooked New Jersey but was still on the Pennsylvania side of things. The main bridge that connected the two states through Whiskey and Ridge on the New Jersey side was one of the tourist spots for people to drive over and walk so they could be in two states at once while over the Delaware River.

Their town was steeped in history, and close enough to where George Washington had crossed the Delaware that they were able to gain revenue on the reenactments for the tourists, thus helping keep their town afloat.

The one main road through Whiskey that not only housed Loch's and Dare's businesses but also many of the other shops and restaurants in the area, was always jammed with cars and people looking for places to parallel park. Dare's personal parking lot for the bar and inn was a hot commodity.

And while he might like time to himself some days, he knew he wouldn't trade Whiskey's feel for any other place. They were a weird little town that was a mesh of history and newcomers, and he wouldn't trade it for the world. His sister Tabby might have moved out west and found her love and her place with the Montgomerys in Denver, but Dare knew he'd only ever find his home here.

Sure, he'd had a few flings in Denver when he visited his sister, but he knew they'd never be more than one night or two. Hell, he was the king of flings these days, and that was for good reason. He didn't need commitment or attachments beyond his family and his son, Nathan.

Time with Nathan's mom had proven that to him, after all.

"You're still daydreaming over there," Fox called out from the other side of the bar. "You okay?"

Dare nodded, frowning. "Yeah, I think I need more caffeine or something since my mind keeps wandering." He pasted on his trademark grin and went to help one of the new arrivals who'd taken a seat at the bar. Dare wasn't the broody one of the family—that honor went to Loch—and he hated when he acted like it.

"What can I get you?" he asked a young couple that had taken two empty seats at the bar. They had matching wedding bands on their fingers but looked to be in their early twenties.

He couldn't imagine being married that young. Hell, he'd never been married, and he was in his mid-thirties now. He hadn't married Monica even though she'd given him Nathan, and even now, he wasn't sure they'd have ever taken that step even if they had stayed together. She had Auggie now, and he had...well, he had his bar.

That wasn't depressing at all.

"Two Yuenglings please, draft if you have it," the guy said, smiling.

Dare nodded. "Gonna need to see your IDs, but I do have it on tap for you." As Yuengling was a Pennsylvania beer, not having it outside the bottle would be stupid even in a town that prided itself on whiskey.

The couple pulled out their IDs, and Dare checked them quickly. Since both were now the ripe age of twenty-two, he went to pull them their beers and set out their check since they weren't looking to run a tab.

Another woman with long, caramel brown hair with hints of red came to sit at the edge of the bar. Her hair lay in loose waves down her back and she had on a sexy-as-fuck green dress that draped over her body to showcase sexy curves and legs that seemed to go on forever. The garment didn't have sleeves so he could see the toned muscles in her arms work as she picked up a menu to look at it. When she looked up, she gave him a dismissive glance before focusing on the menu again. He held back a sigh. Not in the mood to deal with whatever that was about, he let Fox take care of her and put her from his mind. No use dealing with a woman who clearly didn't want him near, even if it were just to take a drink order. Funny, he usually had to speak to a female before making her want him out of the picture. At least, that's what he'd learned from Monica.

And why the hell was he thinking about his ex again? He usually only thought of her in passing when he was talking to Nathan or hanging out with his kid for the one weekend a month the custody agreement let Dare have him. Having been in a dangerous job and then becoming a bartender didn't look good to some lawyers it seemed, at least when Monica had fought for full custody after Nathan was born.

He pushed those thoughts from his mind, however, not in the mood to scare anyone with a scowl on his face by remembering how his ex had looked down on him for his occupation even though she'd been happy to slum it with him when it came to getting her rocks off.

Dare went through the motions of mixing a few more drinks before leaving Fox to tend to the bar so he could go check on the restaurant part of the building.

Since the place had originally been an old stone inn on both floors instead of just the top one, it was set up a little differently than most newer buildings around town. The bar was off to one side; the restaurant area where they served delicious, higher-end entrees and tapas was on the other. Most people needed a reservation to sit down and eat in the main restaurant area, but the bar also had seating for dinner, only their menu wasn't quite as extensive and ran closer to bar food.

In the past, he'd never imagined he would be running something like this, even though his parents had run a smaller version of it when he was a kid. But none of his siblings had been interested in taking over once his parents wanted to retire from the bar part and only run the inn. When Dare decided to leave the force only a few years in, he'd found his place here, however reluctantly.

Being a cop hadn't been for him, just like being in a relationship. He'd thought he would be able to do the former, but life had taken a turn, and he'd faced his mortality far sooner than he bargained for. Apparently, being a gruff, perpetually single bar owner was more his speed, and he was pretty damn good at it, too. Most days, anyway.

His house manager over on the restaurant side was running from one thing to another, but from the outside, no one would have noticed. Claire was just that good. She was in her early fifties and already a grandmother, but she didn't look a day over thirty-five with her smooth, dark skin and bright smile. Good genes and makeup did wonders—according to her anyway. He'd be damned if he'd say that. His mother and Tabby had taught him *something* over the years.

The restaurant was short-staffed but managing, and he was grateful he had Claire working long hours like he did. He oversaw it all, but he knew he couldn't have done it without her. After making sure she didn't need anything, he headed back to the bar to relieve Fox. The rush was finally dying down now, and his brother could just sit back and enjoy a beer since Dare knew he'd already worked a long day at the paper.

By the time the restaurant closed and the bar only held a few dwindling costumers, Dare was ready to go to bed and forget the whole lagging day. Of course, he still had to close out the two businesses and talk to both Fox and Loch since his older brother had shown up a few moments ago. Maybe he'd get them to help him close out so he wouldn't be here until midnight. He must be tired if the thought of closing out was too much for him.

"So, Rick didn't show, huh?" Loch asked as he stood up

from his stool. His older brother started cleaning up beside Fox, and Dare held back a smile. He'd have to repay them in something other than beer, but he knew they were working alongside him because they were family and had the time; they weren't doing it for rewards.

"Nope. Shelly and Kayla didn't show up either." Dare resisted the urge to grind his teeth at that. "Thanks for helping. I'm exhausted and wasn't in the mood to deal with this all alone."

"That's what we're here for," Loch said with a shrug.

"By the way, you have any idea what this seven a.m. meeting tomorrow is about?" Fox asked after a moment. "They're putting Tabby on speaker phone for it and everything."

Dare let out a sigh. "I'm not in the mood to deal with any meeting that early. I have no idea what it's going to be about, but I have a bad feeling."

"Seems like they have an announcement." Loch sat back down on his stool and scrolled through his phone. He was constantly working or checking on his daughter, so his phone was strapped to him at all times. Misty had to be with Loch's best friend, Ainsley, since his brother worked that night. Ainsley helped out when Loch needed a night to work or see Dare. Loch had full custody of Misty, and being a single father wasn't easy.

Dare had a feeling no matter what his parents had to say, things were going to be rocky after the morning meeting. His parents were caring, helpful, and always wanted the best for their family. That also meant they tended to be slightly overbearing in the most loving way possible.

"Well, shit."

It looked like he'd go without whiskey *or* a woman tonight.

Of course, an image of the woman with gorgeous hair and that look of disdain filled his mind, and he held back a sigh. Once again, Dare was a glutton for punishment, even in his thoughts.

The next morning, he cupped his mug of coffee in his hands and prayed his eyes would stay open. He'd stupidly gotten caught up on paperwork the night before and was now running on about three hours of sleep.

Loch sat in one of the booths with Misty, watching as she colored in her coloring book. She was the same age as Nathan, which Dare always appreciated since the cousins could grow up like siblings—on weekends when Dare had Nathan that was. The two kids got along great, and he hoped that continued throughout the cootie phases kids seemed to get sporadically.

Fox sat next to Dare at one of the tables with his laptop open. Since his brother owned the town paper, he was always up-to-date on current events and was even now typing up something.

They had Dare's phone between them with Tabby on the other line, though she wasn't saying anything. Her fiancé, Alex, was probably near as well since those two seemed to be attached at the hip. Considering his future brother-in-law adored Tabby, Dare didn't mind that as much as he probably should have as a big brother.

The elder Collinses stood at the bar, smiles on their faces, yet Dare saw nervousness in their stances. He'd been a cop too long to miss it. They were up to something, and he had a feeling he wasn't going to like it.

"Just get it over with," Dare said, keeping his language decent—not only for Misty but also because his mother would still take him by the ear if he cursed in front of her.

But because his tone had bordered on rude, his mother still raised a brow, and he sighed. Yep, he had a really bad feeling about this.

"Good morning to you, too, Dare," Bob Collins said with a snort and shook his head. "Well, since you're all here, even our baby girl, Tabby—"

"Not a baby, Dad!" Tabby called out from the phone, and the rest of them laughed, breaking the tension slightly.

"Yeah, we're not babies," Misty put in, causing everyone to laugh even harder.

"Anyway," Barbara Collins said with a twinkle in her eye. "We have an announcement to make." She rolled her shoulders back, and Dare narrowed his eyes. "As you know, your father and I have been nearing the age of retirement for a while now, but we still wanted to run our inn as innkeepers rather that merely owners."

"Finally taking a vacation?" Dare asked. His parents

worked far too hard and wouldn't let their kids help them. He'd done what he could by buying the bar from them when he retired from the force and then built the restaurant himself.

"If you'd let me finish, young man, I'd let you know," his mother said coolly, though there was still warmth in her eyes. That was his mother in a nutshell. She'd reprimand, but soothe the sting, too.

"Sorry," he mumbled, and Fox coughed to cover up a laugh. If Dare looked behind him, he figured he'd see Loch hiding a smile of his own.

Tabby laughed outright.

Damn little sisters.

"So, as I was saying, we've worked hard. But, lately, it seems like we've worked *too* hard." She looked over at his dad and smiled softly, taking her husband's hand. "It's time to make some changes around here."

Dare sat up straighter.

"We're retiring. Somewhat. The inn hasn't been doing as well as it did back when it was with your grandparents, and part of that is on the economy. But part of that is on us. What we want to do is renovate more and update the existing rooms and service. In order to do that and step back as innkeepers, we've hired a new person."

"You're kidding me, right?" Dare asked, frowning. "You can't just hire someone to take over and work in our building without even talking to us. And it's not like I have time to help her run it when she doesn't know how you like things."

"You won't be running it," Bob said calmly. "Not yet, anyway. Your mom and I haven't fully retired, and you know it. We've been running the inn for years, but now we want to step away. Something *you've* told us we should do. So, we hired someone. One who knows how to handle this kind of transition and will work with the construction crew and us. She has a lot of experience from working in Philly and New York and will be an asset."

Dare fisted his hands by his sides and blew out a breath. They had to be fucking kidding. "It sounds like you've done your research and already made your decision. Without asking us. Without asking *me*."

His mother gave him a sad look. "We've always wanted to do this, Dare, you know that."

"Yes. But you should have talked to us. And renovating like this? I didn't know you wanted to. We could have helped." He didn't know why he was so angry, but being kept out of the loop was probably most of it.

His father signed. "We've been looking into this for years, even before you came back to Whiskey and bought the bar from us. And while it may seem like this is out of the blue, we've been doing the research for a while. Yes, we should have told you, but everything came up all at once recently, and we wanted to show you the plans when we had details rather than get your hopes up and end up not doing it."

Dare just blinked. There was so much in that statement—in *all* of those statements—that he couldn't quite process it. And though he could have yelled about any of it just then, his mind fixed on the one thing that annoyed him the most.

"So, you're going to have some city girl come into *my* place and order me around? I don't think so."

"And why not? Have a problem with listening to women?"

Dare stiffened because that last part hadn't come from his family. No. He turned toward the voice. It had come from the woman he'd seen the night before in the green dress.

And because fate liked to fuck with him, he had a feeling he knew *exactly* who this person was.

Their newly hired innkeeper.

And new thorn in his side.

Find out more in Whiskey Secrets.
To make sure you're up to date on all of Carrie Ann's releases, sign up for her mailing list HERE.